U...

Divinely Inventive

DIVINELY INVENTIVE

Divinely SHE Publications
P.O. Box 32034
Columbus, Ohio 43232

UNO Copyright © 2018 Divinely She Publications
Cover Design: 3JPMedia
Editor: Danee' Jamese

All rights reserved. No part of this book may be reproduced in any form or by any means without prior consent of the Author, except brief quotes used in reviews.

ISBN: 9781520508085

This is a work of fiction. There are no real-life references in the incidents, characters, or places detailed in this novel.

*This book is dedicated to Mr. LaJuan Eugene Watson.
May you rest in POWER!*

Acknowledgement

I would like to sincerely thank everyone that has encouraged, uplifted and inspired me on this journey. It has always been my dream to have my work published. As that dream becomes a reality, I cannot forget those that have helped me along the way. From the deepest place in my being, I appreciate each and every one of you.

Malachi, you are my REASON!

To all of my readers and fans, I am because of your support. Thank You!

Written with Love and Humility,

Divinely Inventive

Part One

One.

When I think about my brother, Juan, I can't help but be proud to be his sister. See, Juan is a H-Town legend. Him, Kenyon and Marcus really put on for the city. I remember one year, they threw a party that brought all the celebrities out. Hell, I still have pictures with Lil Boosie, Scarface and Slim Thug from that night. Those were the days.

Houston misses those niggas. Everybody knew them as " The Squad". They had respect on these streets, but what made them invincible was the fact that they stuck together when other crews fell apart. We all grew up in Sunnyside. Our neighborhood was rough. Any given day anything could go down.

My parents, Carlos and Maria Gonzales, moved to Houston in 1974. They immigrated to America from Mexico and ended up finding work here. My mother was a housekeeper and she hustled tamales on the side. Papi, on the other hand was a stone cold hustler. As a youngin' he used to transport packs over the border for the cartel. When he got old enough, he started his own operation. Despite his success, Papi ended up with a bad cocaine habit. That's how all of my parents' problems started, leading to Juan having to take over the family's operation.

Born in 1980, Juan Gonzales was special. From what I've been told, my brother always had a sparkle in his eyes. My mother told me that the day he was born, the doctor said he'd bring our family riches. That doctor did not lie. Juan was my parents' pride and joy until I was born in 1986. My father named me Griselda after my Tia, but everybody knows me as Grace.
From day one it had always been me and Juan stuck together like glue. That's until he started school and connected with Kenyon and Marcus. It's funny how my parents never had any other children, but I grew up with so many siblings because of Juan's bond with his friends.

Kenyon, who was almost the same age as Juan, grew up across the street. His mother was a base head, so his Nanny raised him. Mrs. Jones was a beautiful lady. She used to watch all of the neighborhood kids while their parents worked. Her husband died from cancer some years before, so she used the daycare to keep her occupied. Karen Green was Kenyon's mother. She came around from time to time, but never stayed. Kenyon hated Karen and he tried to disassociate himself from her as much as possible.

Marcus's story was a little different from the rest of ours. He moved into the neighborhood when we started Kindergarten. Ironically, he and I were the same age. His mother, Alexis Murray, raised him along with his three brothers; AJ, Shawn and Marvin. They each had a different father and looked nothing alike. Growing up, Alexis was known as the neighborhood hoe. Trying to escape from his mother, Marcus started hanging under Kenyon. Looking at him like a little brother, Kenyon protected Marcus. I remember one time he came to our third grade class and beat Melvin Brown up, who had been teasing Marcus about his mom.

Bottom line- we were family. Sunnyside brought us together, but the struggle, love and loyalty bonded us. The Squad's story is unique.
It's full of highs, lows and mysteries. One thing I do know for sure is the world needs to hear their story. I promised my brother that I'd never let anyone silence them. I'd be responsible for sharing his truth, Kenyon's truth and Marcus's truth. So let me take you back to when everything got started; when they were on the come-up. Shit got real quick.

Two.

I was sitting on our front porch, playing jacks with my best friend Candace. We were interrupted when a black SUV pulled up. Actually, there were multiple cars, but I vividly remember the truck. Several men got out and I recall seeing a lady. She was a Latina. Very well dressed and she had hair like our Abuela's. When they got out, there was a thick tension in the air. I started to see all of the neighbors go into their houses so I knew it meant trouble. Candace and I stayed on the porch as they entered our living room.

"Carlos, we have a problem," the lady stated.

"¿Que?" Papi responded.

"Your shipment has been short the last three rounds. I am losing money. When I lose my money, people lose their lives."

My mother's face turned beet red. My father stood without motion.

"No need for that. We can make it up," my mother responded.

One of the men standing by the door pulled out a pistol.

"I want all of my money returned. You owe me twenty-seven thousand dollars Carlos! No shipments will be made until I am paid in full. Thirty days or your lovely wife dies."

I almost fainted hearing this lady tell Papi she'd kill my mother.

"Comprende," Papi responded as they exited our home.

Once they were gone, I could see that my mother was not happy with my father. She rarely cursed, but she began throwing anything she could find and shouting obscenities in Spanish. I did not know what was going to happen.

About an hour later, Candace and I sat motionless on the porch still in terror. Juan and Kenyon had come from playing basketball and found us sitting in silence.

"What's wrong," he asked in concern. Noticing the look on our faces.

"Papi is in trouble Juan. These people just left and they said they would kill Mamita."

"What people," Kenyon intruded.

"I don't know who they were." I informed them what the vehicles looked like and what I remembered hearing.

"Ken, take Candace home and keep Grace with you. I have to get to the bottom of this."

After we were gone, Juan confronted my parents. He recalled the encounter being really intense.

"Mamita, what's going on?"

"Juan, your father owes a debt. We have to come up with twenty-seven thousand dollars."

"For what?"

"Missing drugs."

Juan was in shock. He always looked up to our father; he couldn't believe he was in this type of trouble.

"Hijo, I need your help. You're sixteen now. The family business needs you. We have thirty days to pay The Osmonds."

Growing up I never met the Osmonds and I never wanted too. The name alone sent chills through people's bodies. They had a reputation for being notorious. Our Abuelo used to tell stories about the Osmonds and we knew they were bad people.

"How do I help? What do we do?" Juan was terrified.

"I have another supplier who will front us. You and I together will move the coke. I need you to help me sell more and make more. Your mother will cut and cook the dope. We just have to move it."

"Juan, your father has a drug problem that he is going to fix," Mamita yelled as she cut her eyes at Papi. "You and only you hold on to the supply. You hear me?"

"Yes."

The year was 1996 and from that day forward, my brother, Juan Gonzales was inducted into the drug game. Papi taught him everything he knew about selling and transporting drugs. Not only was Juan educated, but he had heart. He paid attention to detail. Juan became so consumed in his hustle that he dropped out of school. Worthing High School lost sight of my brother. Juan was so eager to make moves that school was not an option. He was the man and he put us all in position to get money.

Three.

Juan was determined to keep our family safe. When I say he went hard to pay the Osmonds back, I mean that. He sold whatever to whomever. He told me that in the real world, we had to get it by any means necessary. I never forgot that.

The plug trusted Juan and started to give him a heavier load to push after how hard he went with the first shipment. Juan was eager to make more money, but didn't have the muscle to move it. That's when he connected with the person he trusted the most; Kenyon.

Despite being so close to Juan, Kenyon wasn't into anything illegal. He spent the majority of his time on the basketball court and with his girlfriend, Denise. When Mrs. Jones got sick, things got rough for Kenyon. Of course Juan looked out as much as he could, but Kenyon needed to get his own money. I'll never forget the day Juan put him on.

We were all hanging out at The Drop. It was an old park in our neighborhood where we all used to kick it. I was only twelve at the time, so I could only go if I was with Juan or Kenyon. This particular day both Marcus and I tagged along. Juan had just copped a Chevy Blazer and we were all hyped to ride in his whip. It was black with chrome trimmings. At the time none of the other kids had cars, so it was extra lit. When we got to the park, everybody from our hood started showing Juan love.

"Damn J, you really putting on for Sunnyside," Kenyon said with a smile on his face.

"Yeah Lil Bro I do it for my people."

"I want to get down with you. I want to put on for my hood too and take care of Nanny, man."

"Marcus, take Grace to the food truck and bring me back some Chico Sticks," Juan instructed. We knew he didn't want us to hear their conversation. So we eavesdropped on the side of the car.

"Look Ken you're my little brother, my best friend. I don't want you out here man. This game is full of snakes and it's cold. There's no love in it."

"That may be true, but I got you. We can hold each other down. I've been watching you Juan. I can help you move that shit. I heard about that nigga Frank Lucas. They were getting money. We gotta get that kind of bread too, man."

Juan was in deep thought, "What about jail? You willing to bet it all?"

"Hell yeah. I don't have a choice. Nanny sick and Dee is pregnant. A nigga bout to be a dad. I don't have time for no games."

"Word? We gotta go extra hard now man. If it's a boy he better be named after me."

Kenyon laughed, "The only nigga child in the hood named Juan huh?"

After slapping hands their eyes met in agreement and we knew that meant Kenyon was now on Juan's team. Since Marcus was always under Kenyon, that gave me the opportunity to spend more time with him. I know we were supposed to be family, but I always loved Marcus and soon everyone else would know.

Four.

"So, you're stealing my shit?" Juan asked.

"Juan, calm down! He is still your father," Mamita pleaded.

"He ain't nobody's fucking father. He's a base head. He don't protect and provide for us the way that a man should! Mama, can't you see that?"

"Oh you're a tough guy now aye Juan? I taught you everything you know. I am the reason you're on. Don't you ever fucking forget it, hijo."

Juan approached Papi, "If you ever steal from me again, I will kill you. Don't you forget that."

As Juan walked away, Papi grabbed his pocketknife out of his pocket and swung. Before Juan could retaliate, Mama had hit Papi over the head with Abuela's vase that sat on the living room table. Her ashes were inside. Falling to the floor, Papi was severely disoriented. Juan went upstairs and started grabbing all of our father's belongings.

"Juan what are you doing?" I asked as I began to cry.

"He's dead weight. Don't cry Grace he'll never hurt any of us again. Today is his last day here."

Mama grabbed Juan's hand, "Juan, put the things back. We are family. We will get through this."

"Are you serious? Mamita, how long are you going to allow him to keep doing this? He steals, lies, cheats and all you do is protect him. Fuck that! I am the man of this house and I have to protect you and Grace."

Tears flowed down Mama's eyes. "I am okay. We will be fine. You just need to calm down. Your father needs our support right now."

"I can't live in a home with anyone I can't trust. You want him here? Fine, but I'm gone Mamita."

"Detene," Mamita yelled trying to stop Juan, but his mind was made up.

That day our lives changed. Juan kept his word and moved out. Kenyon and Marcus helped him pack and move his things. I was heartbroken. Our entire lives we lived in the same home. Every night we ate dinner as a family. It was hard fathoming life without Juan. It was even harder for me realizing that my father was a drug addict.

Six months after Juan left, Papi died from a heroin overdose. Call me crazy, but I believe Juan saw it coming. He wasn't trying to kick Papi out because he hated him. The truth was he didn't want Mamita and I to experience the demise of a drug addict. Papi was sick and he became more abusive after Juan left. He had hit Mamita several times. I called Juan but he refused to get involved. Instead, he made sure the bills were paid and I had everything I wanted.

Ironically, Papi died on Christmas in 1999. Juan had come over with Kenyon, Denise and Baby KJ. Mamita cooked a multicultural feast. We had arroz con pollo, tamales, turkey, fried chicken, macaroni and cheese, and sweet potatoes. Denise made some southern greens and cornbread. Juan had bought barbeque from Mr. Ribs, the best place to grub in Houston. Everything was going good until Papi woke up looking for a fix. He was grouchy and almost ruined dinner.

"Maria, where is your purse?" he asked.

"Carlos, hoy no es navidad." I could tell Mamita didn't want our company to know what they were saying. However, we all knew Papi was on one.

After putting on his clothes, Papi kissed Baby KJ and I. He walked out the house headed towards the spot. About three hours later, Joe came knocking on the door asking for Juan.

I don't know exactly what he said, but I know that Juan was never the same after their conversation. My brother was always strong, but he was compassionate. It wasn't until my father died that hatred manifested in Juan's spirit. He was no longer Juan from Sunnyside. He became Uno. Unlike Juan, Uno was feared. He was also respected. Sunnyside knew that and soon so would the rest of H-Town.

Five.

It was 2000 and Marcus and I were finally starting high school. Juan had moved Mama and I out of Sunnyside, but we still owned our house so I was able to attend Worthing with all of my friends. By this time Juan and Kenyon were balling. They had matching Lex trucks with the bubbled-eyed lenses. It's funny because everybody thought they were rappers because of how they dressed. I wasn't complaining though. Both Juan and Kenyon made sure I had what I wanted and more. The only problem was they kept me under heavy surveillance. Ironically, the person they had protecting me was the person I needed protecting from.

"Aye, make sure you at my locker after school. Ken supposed to pick us up. If he ain't here we gotta walk so don't be bullshittin," Marcus instructed.

"I got you," I responded as I switched my ass as hard as I could. I ain't gone lie.

I was one of the baddest chicas in Sunnyside. Being a Latina, I was a redbone with long flowing hair down my back. My eyes were green like Papi's. I had nice hips and a flat stomach. Niggas loved trying to get on with me on the low because they feared Juan. I enjoyed the attention, but truth be told, I didn't want anybody but Marcus.

One day after school, Candace encouraged me to tell him how I felt. I was nervous as hell, but I did it and that's when shit got crazy for me.

"Where these niggas at?" I asked Marcus irritated that we were standing outside.

"I don't know. Let's just start walking. You got the key to ya'll crib?"

I nodded and we headed towards Parnell Street where we grew up. When we got into the house, I could tell Juan had been there. He was probably with one of his hoes. He didn't trust taking people to where he lived. Marcus turned on the television and headed towards the fridge. That's when I decided to make my move.

"Marcus!"

"What, G? Why the hell you yelling and shit?"

"I gotta tell you something."

Marcus smirked, "What now Griselda?"

"I want to be with you."

He was silent for a good five minutes. "You mean like be my bitch?"

"Not your bitch Marcus. Your girlfriend like Kenyon and Denise- some real shit."

"Hell naw G! You're like my little sister. Juan would kill us."

Approaching him on the couch, I jumped onto his lap wrapping both of my legs around his waist. He did not resist and before I knew it I was staring him dead into his eyes.

"Are you saying that you just flatout don't like me or you're scared about what Juan might do if he finds out?"

"G, you colder than a motherfucker. I can't front, but I just can't do it. Juan and I are brothers. Them niggas look out for me. I could never be disloyal to him."

His loyalty made me want him even more. I kissed his bottom lip, biting it before he turned his head. "What about if you talk to him?"

"What? You mean like ask Juan if he's cool with it?"

"Yes. He knows I'll be in good hands with you."

"Let me think about it. Until then this little shit you're doing gotta stop, G."

While Marcus lectured me I began unzipping his pants. Before long I had his dick standing at attention. I never gave head before, but I had started watching Juan's porn tapes. I wasn't scared though because I felt comfortable with Marcus. Opening my mouth as wide as I could, I stuck his entire dick in. Of course I gagged damn near biting him. His facial expression was priceless. After slowing down I started to catch a rhythm. I started spitting on his dick as I jacked him off at the same time. Marcus started moaning so I knew he was enjoying it. After about seven minutes, Marcus started to nut. On the porn I'd seen the ladies swallow it, so that's what I did.

"Yo G you're wild," Marcus screamed throwing his hands over his face.

"That means you like what just happened?"

"I loved it for real."

"I'm glad because I love you." I laid my head on Marcus's chest to let him know I was serious. My lips and chin were still wet from his cum. This time he kissed my forehead so I knew the feeling was mutual. We never officially had a conversation about being a couple, but that moment forward Marcus and I were like Bobby and Whitney.

Six.

"Aye nigga, make sure you lock that fuckin door," Juan demanded.

"Shut yo scary ass up," Kenyon fired back.

"You know ain't no hoe in my blood. But aye did you holla at Dee about the move?"

Kenyon shook his head, "She scared shitless, man."

"I know she is, but she's our only hope. We can't trust these bitches out here. They too high risk."

"Naw I know what you're saying bro. She the only bitch in the world I trust. I don't even want her in this for real, but if shit goes as planned nobody will ever be able to touch her."

"Ken if we intercept those keys, we gone be having lunch with Hov ya feel me?"

"I'll work on Dee over the next few days. Speaking of our women, I think Marcus and G got something going on."

Juan laughed. "I peeped that shit too. I see the way the nigga be looking at her. Marcus is family. Normally, I'd bust his ass but G at that age when her pussy getting wet. I'd rather she be with a real nigga like one of us than one of these squares plotting. You just gone have to make sure Dee talk to her and get her on that pill. Can't have my baby having no babies."

"I'm on it! I gotta break out though. Dee on my ass. After you bag that shit up make sure you go get you some pussy nigga. You been acting like a bitch all week."

"Fuck them hoes Ken. I gotta get this money. I'll see you tomorrow."

The next day Denise picked Marcus and I up from school. I was surprised to see her.

"What you doing here Niecey?" I asked.

"Ken and Juan sent me to talk to ya'll."

Marcus was confused, "What's wrong with my niggas?"

"They straight. The problem is ya'll fucking and not having protection."

I looked at Marcus in disbelief. How did they know?

"Yes we all know, including Juan. We just want to make sure y'all using protection. Marcus there are rubbers in that bag. G, we are about to take you to Planned Parenthood to get birth control pills."

Neither Marcus nor I said a word. I was actually relieved I didn't have to discuss sex with Mama. Honestly, we barely talked about anything when I hit high school. All she wanted to do was go to Bingo and fool around with Mr. Livingston, the old man that ran the gambling spot. I didn't give a fuck though. Marcus and Candace were my family.

After we left Planned Parenthood, Denise dropped us off at the house on Parnell Street. Juan gave us permission to spend the night. Marcus bought some movies from the bootleg man and I grabbed some snacks from the store.

Being in love was great for Marcus and I.

Seven.

Denise had arrived at an old abandoned building downtown Houston. Inside, Juan and Kenyon were sitting at a table. On the table were bullet-proof vests, different types of pistols, and some cash.

"Wassup Dee," Juan asked hugging her.

"Hey brother," she responded sitting in an empty chair ignoring Kenyon.

Kenyon knew Dee was upset about having to be involved in their affairs. Regardless of her reservations, she agreed to help them. She was as loyal as women came.

"I have to get KJ in a minute. What's the plan?"

"So basically at 5:30, a young bitch gone be driving the dope in from Atlanta. My people said she's going to be driving some black Mazda joint. She's supposed to meet Looch's bitch at the Holiday Inn on Jackson." Juan stated while showing Dee the pictures of the route.

"What am I supposed to do?" Denise asked.

"After we kidnap Looch's bitch, you're going to pretend to be her and get the dope from the young chick. The money right there is her cut. She should have a Gucci purse with ten keys in it," Kenyon continued.

Denise was nervous, "What if she recognizes me?"

"We got you covered. In that bag I got wigs and make-up. Looch love bunnies so you're going into disguise as a white bitch."

Juan interjected, "Dee. We got everything else covered. All you have to do is get the dope from the bitch and give her the money. Once she's gone you leave the hotel and dump the car on Marvin Drive. One of us will be there to get you."

"What if something goes wrong?"

Kenyon approached Denise, "Worse case scenario just head back here. If you get a bad feeling or feel like something is wrong don't move. We will be in touch with you though. It's a burnout phone in the bag. If you see anybody approach you, crack that bitch in half."

"Dee, I promise we will never put you in a situation we can't get you out of. As long as you've known me, I've always had your back right?" Juan asked.

"Yes, brother. You have."

"We all we muthafuckin got! Let's go get this money."

Denise, Kenyon and Juan parted ways that night not knowing what the next day would bring. The men were filled with adrenaline and Denise with fear. Either way, they were all in and ready to hit the lick.

That night, Denise tossed and turned. Kenyon reassured her that everything would be okay. They had been together since they were in 6th grade. She trusted him and knew that he always had her best interest at heart.

Before it was time for them to leave the house, Kenyon and Denise took a hot shower. When they got out, Kenyon stared at Denise's naked body. He gazed at her, almost piercing her soul.

"What the fuck you looking at Ken?"

"I love you Denise. I want you to be my wife."

"Stop playing games all the time."

"I ain't playing baby. Start planning a wedding. We can have it wherever you want. If you want to go to an island, we're going to an island."

Denise was in shock. "Are you serious?"

"Hell yeah. After we make this move we gone have more than enough bread to do whatever the fuck we want to do."

Wrapping her arms around Kenyon, Denise was on cloud nine. They kissed passionately before putting on their clothes. Kenyon left the house first, meeting Juan at his condo. They checked their connect to make sure everything was in motion.

Despite being street niggas, Juan and Kenyon were smart. They were able to tap into Looch's phone and retrieve all of his phone numbers, including his burnouts. Juan used an application that allowed him to recover all texts and emails. Kenyon went through them all and was able to piece the plan together.

As they'd believed, Looch's Becky was set up at the Holiday Inn waiting on the shipment. Juan was able to break into the room while she was in the shower. When she got out, he informed her to get dressed. He tied her up after taking all of her phones, Ipad, and wallet. Kenyon was outside guarding the premises. He saw several of Looch's men driving by checking out the scene. He made sure no one came in.

At 6:00 the black Mazda pulled in. The girl was black and no older than 19. Denise was there waiting on her. As planned, the two women acted like they were old friends reuniting.

"Jen, how are you," Denise questioned approaching her with her arms open.

The lady hugged her back. Denise could tell she was nervous.

'How about breakfast?" the young lady asked.

Both ladies entered the restaurant adjacent to the hotel. They ordered coffee and ate toast. Making sure no one was looking, they swapped bags. Denise's Gucci bag had the lady's money inside and the young lady's Gucci bag had the kilos.

They nodded to confirm the exchange. After finishing their food and hugging, they parted ways, promising to catch up for drinks later.

While they were in the restaurant, Kenyon switched cars with Denise. He texted her and let her know the keys were inside. Once Denise was gone, Kenyon noticed one of Looch's men sitting in the back parking lot. After texting Juan, they both managed to leave the scene in their disguises.

By the time Looch's crew reached the room the girl was dead and the room was cleaned spotless.

Denise was so relieved when Kenyon arrived at the dump spot. "I can't believe the shit we just did Ken. Are you sure we're safe?"

Kenyon grabbed the duffle bag and torched the hoopty Denise was driving. "Get in and lets roll."

Juan texted Kenyon and made sure they were safe. With all three vehicles and disguises torched, they were in the clear. Kenyon dropped Denise off and went to meet Juan.

"Nigga, do you know what we just did?" Juan gloated.

"Hell yeah! Now, all we gotta do is move this shit ya feel me?"

Juan handed Kenyon a Greyhound ticket. "It's time to hit the road. Moving these keys in Memphis gone be so fire. Niggas around here know what our load is like. We ain't gone change that. Anything we snatch we gotta move out of town so they can't trace it. I know some niggas who sell boy and thirsty to get it. I made sure Looch had no connection whatsoever to anything in Memphis."

'I can do a few drops Juan, but we can't be out of dodge. That's gone be suspect."

"Peep game, you said you were going to propose to Dee right?"

"Yeah," Kenyon was now curious about Juan's plan.

"Take her and the family with you. Play it off like a family vacation. For real you can have Marcus get on the Greyhound with the shit and get it there. I'll stay here and make sure shit flowing alright. Matter of fact, I'll send G with him. That'll really make it believable."

"Bet! Aye, I need you to help me a get a ring though. Something fire too. Dee earned that shit."

"Hell yeah she did…I gotta do something nice for her too. Ya'll got me thinking about settling down and shit."

Kenyon laughed, "Yeah whatever, nigga. I gotta go get some rest. Make sure you go check on G and Marcus. I heard they little asses basically living on Parnell."

"Mamita got her head so far up that old man's ass G basically raising herself. I gotta get ahold of that shit."

"Yeah you do! On another note, nigga how much this shit worth?" Ken questioned.

"If we do right by it, nigga, we can make like six hundred bands. We gone split that shit down the middle and I'm gone throw Dee something from my bag."

Eight.

A few weeks had passed since they busted the move against Looch. Word on the street was, his chick set him up and sadly one of his goons killed her. There were signs and posters all over Houston asking for tips on the murder. Nobody knew who it was, but it sent out a message. Looch was going crazy and everybody was a target because he didn't know where his drugs were. That's when he approached Juan.

"Yo, let me holla at you, Uno," he yelled out the window of his beamer.

"¿Que pasa?" Juan responded getting into the passenger seat.

"You know my old lady got me right?" he questioned.

"I heard. But come on now L, you know these broads can't be trusted. Why you think I don't have one?"

Looch stared at Juan's mannerisms. "I know she sold it to somebody around here in Houston. I'm trying to find my sword. You know anything about that?"

"Come on, nigga. Don't even come around here with that noise. We both know boy ain't my thing. In all the years I been out here I aint never touched it and I don't plan on it. So if you're asking me if I have yo sword, the answer is no."

Looch sensed Juan's agitation. "It's not even like that. I'm just seeing what the streets know. Right now I don't got nothing. I'm fucked up. So, I was wondering if you could front me a chicken."

"I don't front whole thangs. I might can stunt you a half, but even that's outside of what I do, Looch. How soon can you shake back?"

"Juan, I need it man. I can have you all the bread back within like a week. That's my word."

Juan contemplated Looch's promise and decided to help him. He knew it would be good for business, keeping that doorway open. "Ight, I tell you what, I can front you half later on today. I'll have my people get it together. We going on a family vacation. When I come back in a week or so, I expect you to have my money."

"Fa Sho!"

After dapping hands Juan got out of the car. He had an inkling about Looch and couldn't quite put his hands on what his motives were. Either way, he was always prepared. Looch took a major hit and Juan believed he would take anyone down with him, including The Squad.

Despite his reservations Juan had one of his people provide Looch with the product. After the transaction was complete, he informed Kenyon about what had taken place. Both men agreed that Looch was on some bullshit and they were watching him closely.

As planned we all set out to travel to Memphis. Ken and his family got on the plane. Marcus and I took Greyhound after we got out of school that Friday. I was upset that we couldn't take a flight, but I knew there was more to the story.

"Why are we on this funky ass bus and everybody else on the plane?" I asked.

"Shut up G damn! Just enjoy the ride. It's not that bad," Marcus responded.

"You don't have to be rude, Marcus."

Marcus grabbed a notebook from his book bag and doodled on an edge. He handed me the paper and it read: *I got Juan's shit so chill.*

I couldn't believe it. Marcus and I were traveling across state lines with dope. Real dope! At first I almost pissed my damn pants, and then I realized what that meant. Juan trusted Marcus and I. So sooner or later, we would be making money just like them. Now, I know that sounds crazy to even want to be involved, but I wanted in. The only successful people I ever seen sold drugs. I didn't want Juan to always have to take care of me. I wanted my own money and I was going to prove to him that I was worthy.

Nine.

Memphis was amazing. We enjoyed the resort. Juan left us money for shopping and we hit up every soul food spot we could find. I spent a lot of my time with Dee and KJ, while Ken and Marcus made moves. It's funny that Dee was only a few years older than me, but she felt more like a mother than Mamita. We barely spent any time together anymore. I was living in Sunnyside with Marcus and Dee made sure I was straight. Prime example of why I always say that blood doesn't mean shit with matters of family.

Being honest, the vacation really made me appreciate Juan and Kenyon even more. They really put themselves in a position to give us a better life. Who would have known that some dirty kids from Sunnyside, Texas would be living it up in a penthouse resort? I sure as hell didn't. Dee said she always knew one day we'd all have better. I guess God was bringing her dreams into fruition. My prayer was that Marcus would start moving up. I wanted to live like Dee.

Kenyon planned a special family dinner our last night in Memphis. He said it was to celebrate family and loyalty.

"As you know I brought you all here so that we can celebrate our summer. Before we go, I'd like to say a few things to my beautiful lady."

Kenyon turned facing Dee. She smiled as he dropped down on one knee. We all started screaming and clapping.

"Denise, you are my everything. My best friend, confidant, the mother to my seed. I couldn't imagine spending my life with any other woman. As you get ready to finish nursing school, I'd like for us to start a new chapter together as husband and wife. So, a real nigga asking if you'd marry me?"

Full of emotion Denise could barely talk. When she accepted the ring, we all knew she said yes in the midst of all the mumbling. I was so happy for Kenyon and Dee. They were the only couple in the hood that had been rocking since forever. I can't front, I wanted the same for Marcus and I.

"Bae, you see that stone?"

Marcus was dazed. "Hell yeah G. I gotta get my bread up to get you one of those."

"I know that's right! Marcus, we gotta make moves so we can live BIG like them."

He agreed.

I didn't know how much money they actually had, but I knew they were building riches. Juan no longer shopped at the hood stores. He always wore designer clothes and pushed foreign whips. He had bought three condos in Spring Branch, which was very upscale. Mamita lived in the smaller condo, Juan had the middle one with the luxury gate, and Kenyon had the largest one on the block because he had an actual family. Of course I was supposed to live with Mamita and Marcus had a room at Kenyon's, but we loved Sunnyside. The house on Parnell gave us our privacy and access to hood shit. Truthfully, that's all we knew.

Ten.

"What's up with my bread Looch?" Juan demanded.

"Product didn't jump. I'm trying to shake back now."

"Is that right?"

Looch pleaded, "Man you know I wouldn't play you Juan. I respect what y'all niggas do for Sunnyside. Shit, the H period. I wouldn't shit on the home team."

"You know what I hate the most about the game?"

Neither Looch nor Kenyon answered.

"Pussy ass nigga," Juan yelled as he pulled the trigger on his pistol shooting Looch in the head

Blood splattered like a paint ball all over the wall behind where Looch sat. Some stains even reached Kenyon's shirt who was standing on the side of the table. Although Looch was tied to the chair securely, the bullet was so forceful that when his body fell back, it thrusted the chair into the wall. Blood flowed from the hole in his head and corners of his mouth.

Juan laughed as he stood over Looch's body. "K, can you believe this nigga?

"Shit crazy. I can't believe he really thought he was gone lick us."

"Pillow-talking ass nigga. He got Sheree' in the bed and don't even know that's Dee's people. I had a bad feeling when I gave him the pack. He was too thirsty after his hit."

Kenyon pulled out a duffle bag filled with money. "Good thing I went behind him. We ain't take a complete loss on the work. It's 15 bands in here."

"We can put the twelve back for the yay and give Dee and Ree the 3 just for looking out."

"Shit, Dee need to be giving the money to me as much as she in my pockets. I ain't trippin though. She's almost done with nursing school."

Juan sat Kenyon down as if they were not joined by a dead man. "K, I seen you with Nina the other day. You out here foul. Dee been down since day one. For real she really helped us come up from nothing. Don't get sloppy out here over no pussy. Nina cool but she a rat. Dee not only hold you down but she hold The Squad down. She's in school and bout to be making bread all on her own; all legal. Only a fool would fuck that up."

"Bro, I hit her a few times after the club. A few! She have her people tell Marcus she pregnant. I blow down on her to see what's up and she like she knocked and I'm the father. I go down there like it ain't mines and you don't need to have no baby. So she like pay me five bands or I'm telling Baby Dee. I told her she can have the money, but I'm going with her to get the shit done. So that's probably when you seen me."

"Casanova and shit! I told you these hoes scandalous!"

"You ain't never lied. But for real why you telling me about Dee, it's time for yo ass to settle down too. Leslie been waiting her whole life for you and shit."

"Ken, a lady only gone ruin my focus. I can't afford to get caught slippin. Once we out of Texas and poppin bottles at the White House, I'll settle down. In the meantime I'm gone keep tricking with the bust downs."

"Whatever you say, nigga. Just be ready for Atlanta tomorrow. Shit bout to be lit ya hear me?"

"I'm ready. I ain't even packing no bags. It's our time Kenyon. Let's go get this money!"

Part Two

Eleven.

June 3rd 2003, a week before my 18th birthday, I gave birth. Crazy as hell to believe Marcus and I had a baby at only seventeen. We named our daughter Mari Monet. She was dark skinned like Marcus. Her eyes were round and surprisingly hazel. She also had full lips like her father. Mari's hair was exactly the same as mines and Mamita's. Our baby was beautiful and I knew that she would keep Marcus and I together forever or at least that's what I thought.

"G, where you at?" It was Denise on the other end of the phone.

"Hey Dee I'm at home with the baby waiting on Marcus. What's up?"

Dee's voice was shaky. "I'm bout to come get y'all okay?"

"What's wrong?"

"Get dressed. I will be there in about thirty minutes."

I could tell by her voice that something was wrong. Almost an hour later, Dee was at my house picking us up. I thought it was weird considering I had a brand new 2003 Lexus Coupe. Both Juan and Marcus made sure we had everything we needed and more.

When I got in the car, Dee was listening to SWV, which was odd because she only played bounce music. "Denise, what the heck is going on?"

"Not too much baby. I just wanted to see ya'll."

"So why are we leaving the house? I cooked some chicken and rice. We could've had dinner."

I could tell that she was trying to play it cool, but I was anxious as hell. I didn't know where we were going or why. What really tripped me out was when we dropped Mari off to Dee's mother who we all called, "Mama." I mean she watched the baby all of the time, but I had no need for a babysitter. Once Mari was out of the car, I couldn't take it anymore.

"WHAT THE FUCK IS GOING ON?" I yelled.

Denise stopped the car. She grabbed my hands and delivered a blow, "G, Mamita is dead. She had a heart attack this morning. I'm so sorry sis."

I was silent. It was almost as if I was not present in the car. The only thing I could muster up the strength to ask was where Juan was. I needed my brother more than anything and I knew he needed me. When we arrived to Mamita's condo, Juan and Ken were outside with Mr. Livingston. Juan's car door was open and he was blasting Scarface's "Never Seen A Man Cry." He had a bottle of Moet Champagne in one hand and a blunt in another. Ironically, Juan never smoked or drank because he refused to become addicted like Papi. I got out of the car and ran to console my brother.

"She's gone G!" he screamed repeatedly as his tears soaked my shirt.

"What the fuck we gone do now?" I asked now crying myself.

"WE GONE MUTHAFUCKIN BALL!" he screamed hopping on top of his car's hood. I knew he was drunk.

Juan danced for at least another thirty minutes before Kenyon finally got him down. I believed that was his way of grieving. Thank God we had Kenyon and Denise. I mean we didn't know the first thing about funerals or even death for that matter. When Papi died, Mamita handled everything.

Dee made all of the funeral arrangements and Ken tried to keep what little remained of Juan together. Me on the other hand, I was left alone. It had been four days since my mother passed and four days since I laid eyes on Marcus. The day of the funeral he showed his face as we were getting into the family car.

"Baby, I'm so sorry to hear about Mamita," he explained while grabbing Mari.

"Put my baby down, bitch," I exploded. "You ain't been home in days! Four days, Marcus! You ain't dead or in jail so where the fuck you been?" Before I knew it, I was going upside his head. I tried to take his head off with my shoe. I was so angry and hurt. Staying out all night was something Marcus had never done before.

"Are you muthafuckin crazy?" Kenyon asked Marcus as he pulled me off of him. "Now is not the time. They just lost their mother. Get in the fuckin car before Juan kill yo ass over some bullshit."

Marcus didn't say a word. Instead he made sure Mari was safe in her seat and headed to his car. He followed behind the processional and tried to sit in the back of the church. Dee made sure his ass was on the front pew with Mari and I. At that time I didn't give a fuck. Marcus had betrayed me in the worst way possible and I was in no space to forgive him.

At the re-pass I noticed Juan pulling Marcus outside, so I followed behind to see what was going on.

"Where you been man?" Juan asked standing in his face so close their noses were touching.

"I was trying to get this money back."

"What money?" Juan questioned.

"The other day I'm at the spot. I hear a knock on the door. It was Rose, a fiend I always serve, so I let her in. Well apparently some young niggas had her knock on the door. Next thing I know I'm getting rushed by at least four dudes masked up. They let Rose out and tied me up. They cleaned me out. They took the heat, work, money and even my jewels. Shit, they even took a nigga phone. But they didn't kill me. That's how I know it was some young niggas. I heard them call one of the dudes Smoke. By the time I was able to untie myself, I went straight to work looking for Rose. I got that old bitch tied up in the basement as we speak. I'm gone get them niggas."

Juan listened to Marcus talk, but his facial expression showed he was skeptical.

"No lie. By the time I got free and thought about coming to get y'all, that's when I found out Mamita had died and the funeral was today. I ducked off in Sunnyside just to make sure I was safe. I ain't want to take that smoke home."

"Don't ever do that bullshit again, Marcus. You call us anytime shit jump off- flatout. G, is your woman and has your kid. Don't get stupid. They are all I have and I will kill about them. I don't give a fuck about what's going on, don't do my sister like that or we gone have problems. Not only that, but we a fuckin squad. You find us next time some shit go down. I don't give a fuck what it is. "

Marcus pleaded, "Come on now Juan you know I love Griselda's crazy ass. Only way I'm leaving her and Mari is if she kill me or some shit. I'm Squad til I die, nigga. It's always been family first and always will be."

"That might happen. She's loco like Mamita used to be back in the day. Fuck all that though we gotta find these little niggas and let this bitch Rose know just who the fuck we are."

Twelve.

Dee and I always spent our Sundays together with the kids. We cooked and made desserts. Juan, Ken and Marcus attended occasionally when they weren't busy running the streets. This particular Sunday they joined us and it felt good. We hadn't spent family time since Mamita's death.

"What ya'll cook?" Kenyon asked walking in the door full of sweat.

"Dee made smothered chicken, rice, asparagus and sweet rolls. I made banana pudding and a lemon pound cake."

Marcus rubbed his hands together, "Ya'll wasn't playing today."

Although we were still together, I harbored a lot of resentment towards Marcus. Not only had he been running the streets more than he was home, but our sex life went downhill. I hoped that being around Dee and Kenyon would help us get back on track as a couple.

"I get the first plate since I'm the oldest," Juan yelled flopping on the couch next to me. He kissed me on my face at least five times.

"Knock it off Juan. I'm trying to watch the news."

"The news is depressing. I don't see how y'all watch that shit," Marcus intruded.

Just as I was about to flip the channel, the headline read *Sunnyside Woman Dead Family Wants Answers*. As we watched the broadcast, it was devastating. Children and young women were on the television pleading for answers on the murder. The lady's name was Rose James and despite being a drug addict, she was loved. Authorities reported that her body was found near The Drop, burned in an abandoned car. They used her dental records to identify her.

"She look so familiar. Damn that's fucked up somebody did her like that," I stated.

"Oh well they ain't the only ones without a mother," Juan responded.

I changed the subject because I didn't like his energy.

After Ken took a shower we all sat at the table to eat. As we were laughing and talking shit, there was a knock at the door.

"Mark, get the door for me, man. You're the closest," Kenyon said.

There was a skinny white man standing there. "You've been served," he said dropping a letter in Marcus's hand and running off.

"What the hell is that?" Dee asked, but Marcus was silent. He handed the paper to Kenyon and Dee snatched it out of his hand.

"You muthafucker!" she yelled before throwing the paper at Kenyon and heading into their bedroom.

Once they were gone, I picked up the letter and basically it said Little Nina from around the way was accusing Kenyon of being her baby's father. She had a lawyer and a judge issued a warrant for a paternity test. Nina and I were cool, but I couldn't believe Ken was smashing her. I knew she was money hungry, but I also knew she was smart. I felt bad for my girl Dee and I knew that the baby might ruin their relationship.

Thirteen.

"Are you sure you want to do this G," Juan probed.

"Hell yeah. I'm ready, Juan. Damn!"

For the first time in a long time, I saw fear in my brother's eyes. Ironically, I was fearless. Juan needed me and I never even thought twice. Plus, I wanted to make some extra money so I could start separating from Marcus. At the time I didn't necessary want to be without him, but I was unhappy with him. Since having the baby, things had been awkward between us. I started talking to Dee's cousin Ryan on the low just for company. He had started to be there for me in ways that Marcus wasn't.

"You know what to do right? Follow the plan. Get in and out."

"I got it," I yelled rolling up the window.

I pulled off Parnell Street in a 1996 Honda Accord heading to Atlanta. Juan had hooked up with some Russian and they needed somebody to drive their packs. When I got word, I knew that was my move. They paid their drivers by the weight and let's just say this one run could change my life. I not only did it for me, but for Mari. Shit, I learned a long time ago that parents gotta make sure their kids are straight.

"Name?" this manly looking lady asked when I finally pulled up to the spot.

"Zell," I responded handing her the badge Juan gave me. After scanning it, she let me through the gate.

As much as I thought I'd seen, I was sadly mistaken. This place was bigger than a mansion, more like a palace. There were beautiful statues and flowers all over. I knew this man Vlad was stacked. His security was deep as hell. I was directed to a man named Halo. When I finally reached him, he handed me a small zip-lock bag.

"Test," he demanded.

Shit I forgot I lied and told Juan I knew what good product tasted like. I remembered hearing Marcus say it should taste like black licorice. So, I tasted the nasty ass shit and gave a head nod.

"Wait here!"

After five minutes a young woman appeared. She was Russian too.

"Madam, I will now take your vehicle. Follow me please."

"What are you talking about?" I was confused.

"We are switching cars. This one stays here."

Next thing I know, Halo was pulling around an old Cavalier. I don't know what year it was.

"Are you sure I can make it back to Texas in this?" I asked.

"Absolutely! We will be following you in case of any mishaps."

These Russians ain't shit to play with I thought to myself. Hell, I was lightweight shook, so I did what they said.

It took me almost twelve hours to get back to Texas. The entire drive, all I could think about was Marcus and my situation with Ryan. I stopped to eat at Denny's and saw a cute little family that reminded me of what Marcus and I used to have. I knew it was fucked up to be cheating, but Ryan was a cool laid-back type of dude. I liked him because he was a regular guy like Marcus used to be. I wasn't stupid. The Squad had women all over Houston. The only one that didn't get sloppy was Juan.

When I got home from the trip I was all over the place. I was trying to process the business and my relationship drama at the same time. Juan was good at maintaining his emotions so I called him over so we could talk. I needed help processing what the fuck just happened.

"Damn G! I'm so glad you're back. Do you know what you just did for us?"

"Juan, how much money can we make off this shit? I was scared as fuck seeing all them damn Russians and guns!"

"At least three million and that's on the low end Mami! This shit is cavi. Ain't nobody around here moving nothing like this. You have nothing to worry about, I'd never put you in harms way, Hermana."

I felt a little better. "What's my cut?"

"You get a third."

Fourteen.

When I say things changed fast for us, I mean it. After my first trip to get the yay, the Russians started to trust us. Shit, I had hit the road and copped from them at least fifteen times. Juan had our operation on lock. I was the transporter. Juan was the negotiator. Kenyon was the brains. Marcus was in charge of the spot and keeping the little niggas in line.

Since we had bossed up so much, we decided to do a holiday giveaway for Sunnyside. We hired a DJ, entertainment for the kids and catered food. We literally brought Houston out for this event. Although it was meant to be a good time, the haters came out with the supporters.

"You good sis?" I asked Dee when I seen Nina walk up holding her daughter.

"Girl, I'm fine. Kenyon just better keep that thing in line."

I noticed Nina staring at Dee so I went and hollered at Kenyon. Nina didn't know Dee. She was very classy, but could be vicious. Luckily, Nina kept her distance until it was time to take pictures.

When we all gathered to take the family picture Juan wanted, Nina got heated because she felt we were leaving her daughter out of the picture.

"Kenyon, I know you not about to be taking a family picture without my baby!" she yelled.

He ignored her so she yelled again, "Kenyon!" As she started to approach us Juan looked at Kenyon and yelled, "Aye yo K, you better get this bitch man before I smack her."

"Gone with that mess Nina. This is not the time or place for that drama," Kenyon stated firmly.

"Fuck you nigga! Don't ever try to stunt cause yo bitch here. At the end of the day, this yo fuckin daughter."

People started gathering around Nina. Niggas loved drama.

An older lady from Sunnyside named Ms. Jane yelled, "Come on Nina. This day is for the kids. Deal with this mess later."

Nina wasn't hearing anybody. Instead she was yelling and acting a fool. Despite being only five feet tall, Nina was solid. She had really thick thighs and a small waist. In school she was a tomboy and she participated in a lot of sports. Very muscular in stature, I could see her sizing Dee up who remained silent the entire time.

"I'm sorry Ms. Jane, but we gone deal with this now! This hoe ass nigga not about to play my child in front of this hoe."

"You raggedy broke bitch. You want my attention huh? You want everybody to know you're a fuckin cum dumpster huh? Ain't nobody playing Mire. It's you, bitch, that I ain't dealing with. You a fuckin bird. Get yo dirty, begging ass the fuck out of here before you get dropped. Trying to disrespect my woman. She's more of a mother than you'll ever be. Now, I'll deal with you and yo baby when I muthafuckin feel like it."

Nina handed Amire to a younger girl she was with and lunged towards Kenyon as she spat in his direction. Her saliva landed on his cheek. Before he could react, Dee grabbed Nina by her hair and swung her to the ground. Nina tried to reverse the slam, but Dee was too quick. She straddled on top of her and began punching her in the face repeatedly. Blood started to fly from her mouth and nose. One of Nina's friends tried to grab Dee and that's when I snatched her up and threw her to the ground. I wasn't in it, but they weren't about to jump my girl. Besides, Nina needed her ass beat for how she acted.

"Bitch, don't you ever disrespect my man!" Dee yelled as she continued to punch Nina.

Finally, Ken grabbed Dee off of Nina as Juan yelled, "Ken get her man. She gone kill that damn girl."

As Ken carried Dee to her car, she was in an uproar.

"Dee, calm down. This bitch ain't worth it," I assured her.

"Fuck that G. I haven't said shit about this situation because the child innocent. However, I aint for this bullshit from her or this stupid ass nigga." She mugged Kenyon in the face with her pointer finger.

"Bae, I'm sorry! I ain't mean for this shit to happen."

"Yeah whatever!"

When we reached Dee's SUV her people started showing up. Her Aunt Noodles stayed lit. She was always knocking chicks out in the projects.

" Shid G, who the fuck want it? Ya'll know I don't play about my muthafuckin family," she yelled.

I laughed, "Noodles chill out. This ain't nothing we can't handle. Dee beat the shit out of Nina though."

"Good. That young bitch ain't have no business fucking on her man in the first place. Shit."

Dee's sister Rochelle wasn't with the drama. "I don't care what the case may be. Denise don't need to be in the streets fightin over your shit, Kenyon. You need to control your bitches- period!"

"Ro, I'll handle it. Nina just ghetto, but you know I ain't gone let shit happen to yo sister."

Kenyon was wrong. As we stood there talking, Nina and her brother Malcolm approached us. All I remember is seeing Nina's fucked up face and hearing gunshots. I started running and the rest was a blur. When I looked down, I realized that I had been shot in the arm. I didn't feel the pain until I tripped over a rock trying to escape.

"Juan!" I screamed hoping that he was near.

Fifteen.

"What's your name young man?"

"I'm KG."

"Well Mr. KG what can we help you with today?"

Kenyon hesitated. " Look, I don't really pray much. For real I never pray. My lady upstairs in surgery. It's my fault and I need you to ask God to spare her life. I can't lose her. Tell him I'll be a better man to her and my kids. Please just let her make it through this. "

"God knows your heart young man. All you have to do is tell him exactly what you need."

Kenyon placed a hundred dollar bill on the table and walked out of the chapel. As he was leaving two detectives approached him.

"Are you Mr. Green?"

Kenyon didn't respond.

"We're not here to cause any problems. Just trying to get some information on what happened to Denise Jackson."

"I don't know shit," Kenyon responded.

"Now, witnesses on the scene say that she was shot after an altercation with your baby's mama. Do you know anything about that?" the officer questioned.

"I ain't see shit," Kenyon responded.

"Well if you hear anything or your memory comes back, please give us a call," the detective responded handing Kenyon his card.

The fat, black detective was not convinced Kenyon was being truthful, "He knows what happened."

"Sure he does. Fuckin hoodrat," the white cop with the long beard responded.

As they were talking shit the phone rang. "Gazano," he answered.

"What's wrong?" Officer Milford questioned in concern.

"Our suspects, Nina and Malcolm Johnson, have just been found dead on Mound Street in Sunnyside."

Milford was puzzled, "You gotta be fuckin kidding me?"

Gazano shook his head, "It's going to be a long fuckin night!"

Kenyon peeked his head out the door to make sure the detectives were gone before he called for the crew. I was released after being examined and given some pain meds. Dee was still in surgery.

"Bae, you good?" Marcus asked as we headed to the Intensive Care Unit where Dee was.

"I'm just in pain Marc, but these meds helping. I just hope Dee is okay."

Marcus was calm, "She gone be Gucci. Watch. God got her. Dee good peoples. She gone pull through for sure."

"You right."

"When this shit all over I want us to go on a vacation with Mari. Shit been moving so fast we barely do family shit. I thought today like, I could never live with myself if something happened to you. G, I probably don't say the shit enough but a nigga really love you. I don't ever want us to drift apart."

Truth was we had already drifted. Marcus was busy running the spots. I was taking trips and trying to raise Mari in between my moves. Ryan made time for me whenever I wanted to hook up or hang out. I didn't really grieve losing my mother, but I realized sex had become my addiction at that time. It was crazy because my man didn't even know what I was going through.

Dee's room was empty when we arrived. I ended up spotting Noodles and the rest of Dee's family in the waiting room.

"How's Denise?" Marcus asked.

"She started bleeding really badly so they rushed her back to surgery. We haven't heard nothing back yet," Noodles responded.

Mama, Dee's mother, had tears in her eyes, but she spoke softly. "Marcus, I need you to go and find Kenyon and make sure he's alright. He stormed out of here in shambles."

"What about you Mama? Are you okay?" I asked wrapping my arms around her.

"I'll be fine baby. The good Lord gone make sure my child is okay."

She had so much faith and I didn't. I never seen anybody survive a tragedy and I didn't have enough faith to make Denise the exception.

Sixteen

Fortunately, Denise survived and things started to look up, especially businesswise.

"Nigga I can't believe this shit! I started with a quarter ounce of dope to my name, now we here!"

Kenyon smiled, " You feel me? All the fuckin shit we then been through and we on top. Don't get no better than that."

"We did this shit together Ken. Every real nigga in Texas gone know who the fuck we are."

"Speaking of Texas, yo sister ready to leave. She said she likes LA and Atlanta and shit. After all that's happened, I feel like I gotta do whatever makes her happy."

Juan wasn't feeling it. "Nigga Texas made us millionaires and you talking about leaving. Hell naw, we can't switch up bro."

"Nigga I don't want to lose my bitch and my son. She almost lost her life and I'm sure she gone leave me if I don't go. Plus, I gotta get Amire eventually and I think it would be best not to do that in Sunnyside. Nina's family been on that bullshit since she died."

"Naw I feel that. Shit, if you bounce, you gotta go to the A. We'll do numbers with you being down there with the Russians. Shit, that would make the trips smoother and all. I just know ain't nobody else gone hold shit down like you, Ken."

"Juan, this shit we doing ain't supposed to be forever. We gotta start working on getting out. Like opening up some businesses and shit; cleaning up the bread. I been thinking about going back to school for business."

Juan laughed, "Nigga yo old educated ass. I feel what you're saying, but I ain't about that shit though. You the brains and I can just give you my shit to invest that way Mari good for life."

"What about yo own kids though? You don't think it's bout that time. Yo ass almost twenty-five. That's OG status."

"Fuck these bitches, Ken. They full of fuckin drama and games. I don't need that shit fuckin up my operation. Look at what yo bitches then put you through! Yo side bitch tried to kill yo main bitch and then left you stuck with a seed. That shit crazy bro."

"You right! Nina fucked up my whole shit and you told me she would. Dee, been down from day one though. She's loyal and she love a nigga for real. I'm the only one that then had the pussy for real. That's rare. She smart as fuck and she make me a better man. At the end of the day my bullshit damn near ruined her so I gotta do what I gotta do to make her happy."

"You know I love Dee's nutty ass. She definitely earned her stripes."

Kenyon nodded, "Hell yeah."

"I'm with you man…Well, since yo ass turning in the keys, nigga, we might as well enjoy Magic City tonight."

Juan ordered a car service to transport them around the A. They were not only celebrating Ken's birthday, but Vlad got a hold of some boy and wanted Juan to move it in Memphis.

The plan was for me to meet them at their hotel once I landed, but I had plans of my own. Marcus was in Houston handling business and Mari was with his aunt. So, I invited Ryan to come meet me for the night in Atlanta.

"Damn! This hotel nice as fuck," he said as we got on the elevator.

"Wait until you see the room we got. I love the Ritz. Juan got me hipped."

"Speaking of yo brother, do he know we fucking around?"

I gave Ryan a shitty look. "Naw he don't and we should keep it that way."

When we got to the room I thought Ryan saw a ghost. He was looking around the room. His eyes were big as hell.

"This shit plush. Look at the view. I'm gone fuck you overlooking the city for sure tonight Geezy!"

I laughed, "Geezy huh? You ain't about that life!"

"I'm taking you from Marcus lame ass for sure."

"Ryan, I like you and you know that, but Marcus and I are family. That's Mari's dad. Our shit low key rocky, but I don't know what's gone happen."

"I respect all that loyalty shit. Like I said, I want you."

He wrapped his hands around my waist and started kissing me. I knew that nigga was feeling nasty cause he started sucking my fucking tongue. That shit blew my mind. I had on shorts with no panties. He started massaging my pussy while we kissed. Before I knew it he had slid his hand under my shorts and started fingering my wet pussy. I could hear the sounds of my juices as his hand went in and out.

"You like that?" he asked.

"Hell yeah," I moaned.

As he started to nibble on my nipples my pussy got wetter. I felt like I was going to explode. Ryan licked and sucked from my titties down to my pussy.

"Ahhh," I screamed as he bit on my clit.

Ryan whipped his dick out and rammed it in my pussy. "Damn G, yo pussy good as fuck!"

I smiled and laid there enjoying the sex. His dick game was crazy and I knew that we had started something that could've potentially gotten us in trouble. I didn't care at that point because the shit felt so good!

Seventeen

"Good Morning Bae,"

"What's up Ken?"

"I love you," he said as he watched her cook breakfast.

"I know."

Their relationship had been rocky since the shooting. Initially, she had plans on leaving him, but she decided to stay. Regardless of what was going on, he didn't miss a doctor's or therapy appointment. He fed and bathed her. He even took care of KJ and the house.

Kenyon spoke with so much authority, "Now that you're feeling better, I think it's time to get married. I been thinking about that island."

Denise turned around and faced Kenyon, "Do you really think we're ready after all that's happened?"

"Come on Bae we then been through hell and back. I know we're still young so that's normal. I just feel like we can make it through anything. I don't want anybody else."

"What about Amire?"

Kenyon paused unsure of how to answer Denise. "I mean that's my child. I ain't no real nigga if I leave her out here and her momma dead."

"I don't know if I can accept that right now, Kenyon. I want us. I want our family. So much has happened surrounding this child."

"I made the mistake, Dee. Amire is just an innocent child. You got my word I'll never cheat again and I'll do whatever I can to make you happy. I'll even leave Texas. I just need you to at least try to give her a chance."

Dee started tearing up remembering what she endured. "Look, I am willing to at least try. However, if I do that then I need something from you, Kenyon. Not just moving but I am ready for you to get out the dope game."

Kenyon gave her a look of confusion.

"Yes, I said it. We are not hurting for any money. Truthfully, ya'll need to start cleaning it up anyway. Maybe open a business or invest in something."

"Bae for real, I'm with you on that. I just gotta convince Juan, Marcus, and G that's the next move for us."

"Speaking of G I gotta call her ass. My Teedy said she was over my sister's house with Ryan the other day."

Kenyon shook his head. "I'm not surprised. She just better be careful cause Marcus been on one lately. I don't even think he worried about Juan. He ain't nothing to fuck with out here."

"Alexis fucked Marcus all up! I can't believe her old ass got popped in a fuckin prostitution ring. That shit is ridiculous. KJ would never see me out here like that."

"I know. That's why I'm marrying you, Dee. You're cut from a different kind of cloth."

"Whatever nigga! You just want these good meals and good pussy I know what's up!"

"Yup! I want all of that forever. So, find an island and let's get busy. Our theme should be some shit like going Green. We about our last name and our money."

Denise laughed, "Ugh Kenyon that's so ghetto."

"So what's wrong with that? I'm a mothafuckin hood star!"

Eighteen.

"G, where you been?"

"I had some business to handle."

"What kind of business? We ain't have nothing to run today," Marcus replied.

I was confused because he never really questioned me before. "Bae, I was in Sunnyside. You know I'm helping Dee get ready for the wedding."

Marcus gave me an emotionless look and then grabbed me by my hair. "Bitch, you must think I'm stupid."

"Get yo fuckin hands off of me! Are you crazy?" I yelled.

"You think niggas don't talk? I know you been fuckin Ryan, hoe!"

I was caught and as much as I didn't want to own my shit, I couldn't lie. Before responding I paused, trying to make sure I didn't say the wrong thing because Marcus was heated. "I'm sorry! I never meant to betray you! It just kind of happened when we were beefin!"

"G, straight up- you ain't shit. You look me in my eyes daily knowing you fuckin another nigga. Let me be fuckin another bitch tho! You lucky I'm not beating yo bitch ass right now! Only reason I'm not is cause I can't be mad that my bitch fuckin a fag. You played yourself."

"Who a fag?"

Marcus started laughing, "Oh you ain't know? Yo boy Ryan just got caught fuckin some little nigga. He wouldn't give the nigga no bread so he outted him! If you were on yo toes in Sunnyside, you'd know that shit! It's all around the hood!"

I was speechless. I knew Marcus wasn't lying because I could see the embarrassment in his eyes. Not knowing what to say, I approached him trying to hug him. "I'm sorry Marcus. I'm so sorry."

He rejected my advance. "You right about that. You a sorry ass mother and a sorry ass bitch."

"Hold up! Fuckin another nigga makes me a terrible girlfriend, but it has nothing to do with Mari!"

"When do you have Mari? You either on the road, chasing Ryan, or somewhere else shopping. I run dope houses and I have her more than you do! Do you see Denise out there like that? Hell no! She get in where she fit in and she stay in her lane. You wanted this though! I thought once we had Mari you'd get yo mind right, but you did the opposite. Me, Juan and Ken know how to stay in the game. This shit don't run us; we run it. You got sucked in and I don't want no bitch that's willing to risk it all for some fuckin money! So you go fuck yo fag and get yo dough. I'm leaving this bitch and I'm taking my daughter. We done!"

His words stung. Tears flowed from my eyes as I watched him pack his things and head out of the door. I wanted to stop him, shit, I even wanted to fight, but I didn't move. There was something about his tone that let me know Marcus's mind was made up about us. He no longer considered us family. I lost everyone I loved besides him, Mari and my brother. At that moment I realized that I had lost him too.

I replayed a conversation in my head that I had with Juan some years before. He told me, "Loyalty is everything! Never be disloyal to the ones who have always had you."

I fucked up and I knew that it would affect our crew.

Nineteen.

Once Marcus and I broke up, things started to get crazy. One of our spots had got hit and one of our shakers in Memphis had been arrested. Word on the street was he took a deal, which included him giving up Juan. We hadn't heard nothing from the law, but it had us shook. The only thing that saved us was Ken and Dee's wedding. It gave us some time to duck off and come up with a plan. Truth be told, we all needed a vacation anyway. The dope game had been good to us, but it was starting to show it's other side.

Dee had planned for us to leave Texas a day early so we could just chill before the wedding shenanigans. Kenyon and Juan stayed in Texas to finish handling business. When we landed in Cabo, Mexico, I couldn't believe how beautiful it was.

"Dee this shit is lit! This place is beautiful."

"It is. I'm so happy we are here. Texas been too much for me lately. I just want to enjoy my family and my man."

"I know that's right. You looking damn good too. How much weight have you lost?"

"Sixty pounds, bitch. I'm making my ass clap all weekend roun' here," Denise clowned.

"Noodles, what's that dance you doing?" I asked. Denise's aunt was in the corner jamming and there was no music on.

"The oddle from a bish named Noodle! Straight Sunnyside shit ya dig!" she yelled.

"Already!" We all giggled.

"Well ladies, tonight is our night. I have dinner reservations at 6 in the ballroom. Sorry to leave ya'll, but this bride needs a nap. I'm gone get a few hours in before the turn up."

Once everybody was gone, I decided to call Marcus to check on Mari. I knew they were coming to Cabo, but I didn't know when. Normally, we would just text, but I called him from the hotel phone hoping to hear his voice and talk to Mari.

"Yo," he picked up the phone.

"Hey Marc, is Mari with you?"

"Naw, she at the shop getting her hair fixed for the wedding."

"Who is she with?" I asked annoyed that Marcus wasn't there with her.

"Does it matter?"

I paused for a minute trying to hold my composure. "Look I ain't call for all of that. I just want to talk to my child and make sure she straight."

"She's good G and you know that. I ain't never gone let her be otherwise. The fuck you thought?"

"Marcus, I never said she wasn't good with you. Regardless, I'm still her mother and I have a responsibility to make sure my little mama good."

"I hear you. You'll see her tomorrow."

Marcus had really pissed me off being so rude. I knew it was time to end the conversation. "Ight, I'll see ya'll when ya'll get here."

As I was hanging up, Marcus interrupted me. "Aye G, ummm I want to let you know that I'm bringing somebody with us tomorrow."

"Somebody like who, Marcus?"

"My lady. She's cool and Mari likes her. I don't want it to be no shit. It's Ken and Dee's day; that's why I'm telling you."

"Marcus, you would really disrespect me and bring another bitch all the way to Mexico with all of our family and friends? Like seriously?"

"Yup. When we had a family your ass didn't want it. You made yo decision when you started fuckin Ryan so you can't say shit about what I'm doing."

"Marcus, you got me fucked up. Don't bring that bitch down here," I yelled hanging up the phone.

Keisha, Dee's baby sister, over heard me yelling and stepped into my room.

"G, you good?" she asked.

"I don't know, Key! Marcus on some straight bullshit."

"What he saying?"

Tears started running down my eyes, "He talking about he bringing some bitch down here with them tomorrow. Like I can't do shit about it because I ruined our family."

"He's talking about Ryan?" she questioned.

"Yeah. How you know?"

Keisha grabbed my hands. "G, we all know what happened! You were wrong. I love my cousin, but he ain't shit. You don't fuck up yo family over a nigga that don't have shit to offer. Real spill."

"I know. Can I ask you something?"

Keisha smirked her lips, "Of course girl!"

"Ryan be fuckin niggas?"

I could tell she was hesitant. "It's a rumor. I wasn't there so I can't say for sure, but a gay boy did have some texts that he put out supposedly from Ryan. Some of my people believe it and others don't. I really don't know, but if I were you I'd get checked out. Ryan is nasty as fuck and will fuck anything. For real G, you need to stop messing with him all together. Try to get your shit together so you can work it out with Marcus."

"He don't want me no more, Key."

"Girl that nigga foolin'! Ya'll been together how many years?"

I had to think back. "Shit we been together since we were kids for real. It's been almost eight years."

"That's a long ass time, Griselda. Marcus loves you. Believe that. He's just hurt. Men are prideful and deal with their shit differently that's all. As a woman, you have to give him something to come home to. Stop being in the streets so much. Get you a little job or legal hustle and show him that you're growing. Marcus got into the game by default. He's a good nigga, G. You just gotta tighten up."

I hugged Keisha so tight after our talk. She always had my best interest at heart. As crazy as it was, all I really had was their family. My only biological family was Juan. He was a man and wild as hell. His advice was always about money. I appreciated the fact that I had Denise and her people.

Twenty

"Are ya'll crazy?" I yelled opening up the door to Juan and Ken standing there in their sombreros.

"Wake ya'll asses up!"

"Juan, would you shut the fuck up? Everybody still sleep!"

Ken was looking around our suite. "G, ya'll bet not had of corrupted my wife or I'm fucking something up."

"You ain't gone do shit, nigga. She upstairs sleep though. The room all the way at the end of the hall is hers."

The resort had brought breakfast so I asked Juan to meet me outside on the terrace so that we could talk.

"¿Hermana que pasa?" he joked.

"I miss you!"

"G, don't start that emotional shit."

"Seriously! Being here with Dee and her people made me realize that you're the only real family I have. Marcus trying to take Mari from me and I feel like I'm losing everything."

"You know I be on the move, but we switching shit up so I'll have more time to spend with y'all. You know I love you though. Everything I'm doing is for us. I want to make sure I finish what Papi started!"

"How much longer do you plan on doing this though? I was talking to the ladies and I gotta do other things Juan so that I can be there more for Mari. You know this nigga Marcus called me a fuckin deadbeat mother?"

Juan laughed, "He wildin out lately man. I feel him though, G. How you gone start fuckin around on the nigga in our hood though? The only reason you ain't dead is because you're my sister. We don't tolerate disloyalty-period. You hurt my nigga and he got every reason to flex on you like he doing."

"I know I fucked up, but I don't think he should leave me over that! We got a family and a daughter. This hoe ass nigga talking bout he bringing some bitch down here. Juan, I'm gone end up having to kill this nigga!"

"Chill out, G. Marcus is family. He's proved his loyalty for real. You just gone have to let this shit ride and get focused on the money. I need you on yo shit."

There I was telling my brother I was hurt and needed to change my life and he had plans to keep me entangled in the chaos. "What do you mean?"

"We gone open up some businesses and shit. Ken talking about a beauty and barbershop and some type of soul food joint."

I was relieved. "Oh so you want me to run the businesses?"

"Something like that! I want you to go get your GED and get a beauty license. That way you can get tax returns and shit. I want you on that ASAP cause we expanding our territory."

"To where?" I asked.

"Baltimore for sure and I'm looking into a little city in Ohio called Youngstown too."

"Don't you think that's doing too much considering that shit about dude in Memphis?"

"Naw, that nigga ain't making no noise. The time is now, G. We gotta get ours so we can get out. A nigga sounding like Ken, huh?" Juan joked.

The others started coming down the stairs so we stopped talking about business. I was not feeling the expansion. I was comfortable with my routes to Memphis and Atlanta. Shit, I even felt protected knowing Vlad was always looking out. Juan's mind was made up and I knew I needed to talk to someone with some sense about my reservations. After the wedding, it was time I sat down with Kenyon. He never lied to me. I also knew he was looking for an out too based on my conversations with Dee on the plane.

As I was sitting on the terrace in deep thought, I heard a tiny, squeaky voice scream, "Tio!" It was Mari running into Juan's arms.

"Mamas," I yelled running through the door ripping my baby from my brother's arms. I kissed her and tickled her at the same time. It was like I needed her spirit to calm mine.

"Look at auntie's baby," Dee said rubbing Mari's curls. Her hair was braided neatly into two ponytails with curls. She even had rhinestones on her braids.

"I know Dee; my baby cold. She gone be the best flower girl in the world."

Marcus flexed his muscle, "She get it from her pops, feel me?"

"Shut yo ass up fool. She is your twin though, but I think she got G's flavor," Dee joked.

"Ya'll gotta chill with all this emotional shit though. Everybody know Mari is fly because of her uncle. Anyway, what's the move?"

Kenyon shook his head. "Y'all a trip! Dee, I have an afternoon planned for you and I. Everybody we will catch y'all at dinner. Enjoy the resort and each other! Be back here at about six for the rehearsal dinner. Please be the fuck on time! I am paying by the hour."

"Marcus, can I holler at you real quick?" I approached him as everyone dispersed. I was holding Mari so he had no choice but to come chat with me. I headed to my room and he followed.

"I was thinking that we could take Mari to the beach and Dee said they have an aquarium somewhere around here."

He shook his head. "G, you and Mari can do that. I have to wait on my guest. I already made plans. I figured you'd want Mamas to stay with you anyway."

"Damn Marcus, are you still on that shit? I told you I was sorry. I am sorry for cheating on you. I get you're mad, but why now? This is not the place for this revenge shit!"

"It's not about revenge, Griselda. I'm moving the fuck on with my life just like you did. I'm dating this girl and she's going to be around so you might as well get used to it."

I sat Mari on the bed. "I ain't getting used to shit. I love you Marcus. I'm not about to accept you and some other bitch. I will beat her ass and ruin the entire fucking wedding if she shows up. I put that on Mamita and Papi!"

"So you'd really ruin they shit trying to clown over some nonsense?"

"Nonsense? You're trying to take my family away from me, Marcus. All I have in this world is y'all! I can't lose anymore members of my family. Fuck that! You bring that bitch up here and it is gone be a muthafuckin problem. I will kill her!"

"That's what the fuck I be talking about. Your daughter here and you worried about some bitch. Grow up G, for real. I'm gone do me regardless. I love Mari and I love yo simple ass too, but I'm not coming back to you cause I can't trust you."

"What do I have to do? I want to fight for us! I promise I wont do nothing else disloyal. I need you."

I could tell I was hitting a nerve because he refused to look at me. Instead he stood facing the door. Before he walked out, he looked back at me and said, "I don't know, G. I need some time."

"I'll give you all the time you need. Just please don't give up on us. At least not yet. This place is beautiful. I just want us to enjoy it together like we always planned."

"She's coming, G! Let's just figure this shit out once we get home. It's Dee and Ken's day tomorrow. Our drama shouldn't ruin their shit. If you love me, then just respect what a nigga asking you. I promise we'll talk when we get home."

Twenty-One.

Saturday, July 16, 2005, Denise and Kenyon became one. They were married in Cabo, Mexico at the Pedregal Resort. The beach was decorated with peach and white roses. Denise wore a custom Versace gown. It was floor length accompanied by a crystal train. All of the bridesmaids wore peach Versace mid-length dinner dresses, with Swavorski crystals on the straps that matched Dee's train. Kenyon and the groomsmen wore white linen Versace two-piece suits with peach button-ups that matched our dresses. KJ was the ring bearer and he wore a white tux with a peach flower. Mari walked down with Amire and they were dressed in white dresses with peach flowers embroidered across the front. The entire wedding party was fly, but no one was as stunning as Denise.

To the surprise of the guests, Kenyon hired Musiq Soulchild, whom he had met in Atlanta, to serenade Denise as she walked down the aisle. He sung his smash hit "Love." When she arrived at the altar, Kenyon was standing there in tears.

She gave her vows first, "Kenyon, sometimes it feels surreal to love someone as much as I love you. My life has forever been changed because of our love. Words cannot describe how much our family truly means to me. You and KJ are everything I've ever needed. As we begin this next chapter, I open my heart to loving and understanding you more. To being your shoulder in any situation. Your voice when you're voiceless. Your calm in the worst storms. Your everything even if we have nothing. I vow to love you from the depths of my soul until my heart no longer beats."

Juan slapped Ken on his back to hype him up to give his vows. He was an emotional mess.

Finally he spoke, "Denise you are the illest chick I've ever known. You are not just beautiful, but you're intelligent and loyal. Our son is blessed to have such an extraordinary woman as his mother. Everyday I thank God for creating you. I understand that I wouldn't be me without a woman like you. You make me better everyday by simply being you. Throughout everything we've been through, you have stood solid. I dedicate my life to loving you, protecting you, and providing for you. Baby, I love you from my soul and I'll continue to love you as my Queen for the rest of my life. Thank you for loving me and gracing me with the honor of being your husband."

By the time Kenyon was done with his vows, we were all in tears. The moment was magical like some shit off TV. The entire time Ken was talking I was staring at Marcus. I knew his little girlfriend was in the crowd, but I didn't give a fuck. I wanted him to know that I was serious about our love and our family. I wasn't gone let nothing get in the way of that.

When the reception started, I noticed Juan looking really sad. I approached him just to make sure he was straight.

"Bro, you good?"

"Yeah I'm good, G. Why you ask that?"

"You just look kind of like something is bothering you. That's all."

He wrapped his arms around me. "I'm good baby sis. I'm happy for Ken and Dee. My nigga really love his lady. I just know that things are about to be different for us that's all. We've always been family and now he has his own family you know?"

"At the end of the day, that's the goal for us all Juan. We all deserve love. Shit, we got the money, now we gotta find people to share it with. You next!"

"Hell naw! I'm marrying my fucking money. It's gone be Sunnyside and The Squad til the day I muthafuckin die. My life is in this shit for real!"

I laughed.

"G, I ain't bullshitting. I'm bout to turn it up on these niggas. Watch. We gotta take this shit to another level before we get out the way. We got the plug, we got loyalty, we got heart and we got a lot of bread to go get!"

I drug my crazy ass brother to the dance floor as he ranted on. I laughed but I knew he was serious. Juan had made it up in his mind that he was devoting his life to the game. That scared me because I was starting to want more for Mari and myself. I was only nineteen and had a lot of living to do. Hell, I think we all were at the place. Well everybody but him.

Part Three

Twenty-Two.

When I tell you we entered 2006 with a vengeance, I mean that. After the New Year hit, we opened up a beauty bar in Sunnyside. Both Marcus and I were in school finishing our licenses as planned. Dee did all of our paperwork and found us some scholarships so we wouldn't have to pay for the schooling. Aside from that, Juan and Kenyon had purchased a building in midtown Atlanta and North Memphis. They were working on opening their Hispanic soul food spot; Mamita's. Shit was going smooth as planned for us, so we decided to celebrate. Juan was turning twenty-six and wanted to do it big.

"G, I need ya'll to find somebody to plan this shit," he instructed.

"You better ask Dee. You know I don't know shit about event planning. I think her home girl from Dallas be doing it."

"I'm gone have Ken holler at her for me, but shit how school going?"

"It's going cool for the most part. I like doing hair and shit. I just don't feel like I have enough time to actually commit to it."

Juan gave me a hard look, "You can't quit. We got a lot riding on this, G."

"Did I say I was quitting? What y'all gone have to do though is get me some help on these roads. Shit! I gotta go to Baltimore on Sunday and then got a final on Monday. How the fuck am I supposed to study and make that long ass trip, Juan?"

"Look, just go to Baltimore Friday night. You can study in the hotel and then once you make the pick up Sunday, you'll already be on point for your test."

"That's not a bad idea. I just gotta make sure Marcus is cool with that because he has Mari."

"He know what you gotta do. Shit it ain't gone be no issue."

I texted Marcus to let him know I wanted to meet up. He was on it. Things had been better since we got back from Mexico, but I wanted more. I knew he was still fucking that bitch he brought to the wedding, but I wasn't really tripping. He loved me and at the end of the day I loved him too. I knew that we would eventually get back together, run our shop and raise Mari. That's what really kept me going.

"I'm about to meet up with him now so I can see Mari before I leave. So, have the bread in the safe at my house before like five on Friday with all the routes and shit so I can look over it before I shake."

Juan smirked, "Look at you trying to be on yo boss shit! I see you, G!"

"My brother is a fuckin Kingpin. I learned from the best," I joked.

"Damn right!"

After hugging Juan and getting a few dollars off of him to take Mari shopping, I headed to Sunnyside to meet Marcus. When I arrived at Pappadeaux, Mari and Marcus were waiting inside.

"Mama!" I yelled grabbing her out of the booster seat. She kissed me with her wet lips, while wrapping her little arms around my neck.

"Marc, what's good?" I asked glancing out the corner of my eyes at him. Marcus was dressed in a Burberry button-up with short sleeves. He had diamond studs in both ears that matched his pinky ring. I even noticed he had on maroon Burberry loafers to match his shirt. I was impressed. Not only was he looking good, but he smelt amazing too. Shit, being honest I wanted to pull his pants down and fuck the shit out of him at that moment.

"I ordered you some hot wings and a Sprite. How you feeling today?"

"That was nice of you. I'm okay, I guess. Getting ready to hit the road to Baltimore in a few days."

"Why you looking like that? Juan said this a big move for us on the illys. Shit for real, we got everything on lock but those."

The waitress had arrived with our drinks. I stirred my pop with the straw as I contemplated what I was getting ready to do. "Yeah he told me all about it. The thing is I have to leave a few days early. I told him I had finals next week and needed to be ready. That's a long trip and I'll be cutting it close. So, I'm gone go early and just study at the hotel. I just need to make sure you got Mari."

"Of course I got her, G. Dee asked for her this weekend anyway. They are taking the kids to some waterpark and wanted her to go with them."

"I guess I'm the last one to know everything."

"Naw, Ken just called as we were pulling up here. Chill out!"

I quickly changed the subject noticing that bitch Bianca was calling his phone. He ignored her call cause I'm sure he knew I was not for the bullshit. "I see she still calling. You ain't stopped fuckin her yet?"

"We ain't about to talk about that right now, G."

"So apparently my feelings still don't matter. I keep telling you time and time again, I want us to work through this. One minute you on it, the next minute you're shutting me down. Come on now Marcus what the fuck?"

He started playing with Mari, ignoring my rant. Of course I was emotional as hell so I shed a few tears. When he saw me crying that's when he started to at least show concern.

"Stop crying, G I'm gone come home eventually. I just gotta make sure you're ready. For real because if you cheat on me again, on Mari I'm killing you and that nigga. I see you trying to get yo shit right. Just know if I come home ain't no more trips and shit. All I want you to do is run the shop and raise Mari."

"Okay," I responded wiping my tears.

There was an awkward silence, "Bianca is pregnant. I can't come home with that hanging over my head. Let me get her through this abortion first. If we gone do this we gotta have a clean slate."

My eyes tripled in size. I was crushed. I couldn't believe that Marcus had made another baby. I was speechless. I wanted to kill them both in that moment, and then I remembered he was out there because I pushed him out there. I knew I fucked up and would have to pay the price.

Twenty-Three.

When I arrived in Baltimore, I had a weird nervousness over me. I couldn't text or call anybody so I said a little prayer under my breath like Mamita used to do. Juan had set it up for me to meet some girl he fucked with named Niv. I didn't know her, but he thought she was solid. Her people were supplying the pills. Juan sent her the bread. All I was supposed to do was pick up the product. When I pulled up on Monument Street I was tripping. Sunnyside was the hood for sure, but this was something different. As I was waiting on Niv, two crack heads knocked on the window asking for dope and everything. I knew I had to get the fuck out of Baltimore.

After about a half hour, I started to get nervous. Normally, all of the drops went down on time, damn near to the minute. As I started to pull off, I was cut off by the police. There was a cruiser in the front and back of me. First thing I did was snap the burner phone in half and stash the pieces in the crack slit in the floorboard.

"Put your hands in the air," the cop yelled as he approached my window with his pistol pointed. I threw my hands in the air and he opened the door. His partner was opening the passenger door at the same time. He grabbed me out of the car and threw me down on the ground. I couldn't see anything but feet moving. I heard a lot of yelling, which is how I know they were searching the car.

"Who sent you here?" the cop questioned as he walked me to the back of the cruiser.

"I have no idea what you're talking about, sir," I responded. Honestly, I didn't have much information to give. Juan always kept it that way. Except for the drugs, we always rode clean. The car I was driving was a rental out of Baltimore under a business. The way I seen it they had nothing on me, or at least that's what I thought.

Once I was taken to the police station, they put me into an interrogation room. What's crazy is they never read me any rights or said I was under arrest. That let me know they only wanted information, and I didn't have nothing to give them.

"What's your name?" the female cop asked. I didn't respond.

She became snippy. "Oh so you're one of them huh? Tough bitches who think they are above the law. Let's see if you're still so tough when you're doing life in prison."

"Am I under arrest?" I finally asked.

"Did you do anything to be under arrest?" she responded.

I didn't answer her question, instead I asked for my lawyer. Juan had taught me what to say, "I am not making any statements without any legal representation. If I am under arrest, please provide me with my charges and an attorney. If not, I am requesting to be released."

The bitch rolled her eyes and walked out of the room. I knew she was on some bullshit. When she came back, she had another cop with her. They were holding a folder with Nadia Gomez written across the top. I figured that was Niv's real name.

He spoke, "You are here because we believe you are connected to Nadia Gomez. Ms. Gomez was apprehended today and we were informed she had a meeting where you were sitting. We are giving you the opportunity to give us any information you may have right now and save yourself. The charges against Ms. Gomez are severe and any accomplice of hers will be charged as well."

"I do not know Nadia Gomez and I want my lawyer now!"

I sat in a holding cell for about three hours before I finally got my call. I didn't want to call Juan directly, so I used our back up. I called Denise's burner instead. She always kept it on her in case of an emergency.

"This is Diane," she answered which let me know she was up on game.

"Ms. Diane, its me, Lynn. I am being held in a Baltimore jail. They have not officially arrested me, but they are holding me because they are saying I was meeting someone they arrested. I don't know what they're talking about nor do I have any more details. Can you send me a lawyer please?"

I heard the concern in her voice, "I'll get right on it, Lynn. Sit tight. I got you."

I knew that meant she was going to get Juan. I couldn't call her back because the plan was to always break the burner phone once we used it. So I knew it was a waiting game. I rolled myself into a fetal position and tried to go to sleep. Ironically, I wasn't nervous or anything. I knew they didn't have shit on me. However, it did intensify the feeling of wanting to get out the game altogether. Marcus and Dee were right. That shit wasn't fit for a mother.

Besides one raid, we had all been fortunate enough to never have any real run ins with the law. Juan thought we were invincible. I thought we were just lucky. Our setup was solid, but sooner or later I knew that luck could run out.

Twenty-Four

"Why the fuck is Dee calling so much, Ken?" Juan asked as they were at the spot waiting for me to call.

"Something might be wrong. Give me a burner so I can answer her," Kenyon demanded.

Denise was in shambles, "Bae, where are you?"

"I'm at the spot what's wrong?"

"I'll be there in a minute," Denise said before abruptly hanging up the phone.

Less than ten minutes later, she was walking through the warehouse door. Both Juan and Kenyon knew that something was wrong based on her demeanor.

After refusing to sit down, she started giving them the run down, "Ya'll the Baltimore Police have G. She called my burner and said she was being detained but hadn't been charged. They claimed she was meeting a woman they arrested and they wanted to know why. She refused to talk, said she ain't know ol' girl and asked for a lawyer."

Juan started pounding on the desk, "JODE! JODE! JODE!"

"Calm down bro. G's solid as they come and they obviously don't have shit. We just gotta call the Jews and get them down there to get her. She gone be straight."

"What about Niv though? If they got her she could give us all up shit! Vlad hooked me up with her so I gotta get with him ASAP. That bitch knows too much and if she breaks, shit can get real for her. We might have to fuck around and kill her whole family."

Kenyon became annoyed, "What the fuck are you talking about, Juan?"

"If that bitch snitch, we wiping out her camp."

"Nigga, I'm not killing no fucking old people and kids. You're tripping. For real, she ain't gone give us up cause we fuck with Vlad. That nigga a different animal. He ain't to be fucked with and everybody know that. So just chill the fuck out bro so we can process this shit and get G home!"

Juan gave Kenyon a stale face and then approached him, "You going pussy on me nigga? This what the fuck we do, Ken! What the fuck you on?"

"I ain't never went pussy on you nigga and I never will. I'm not getting stupid with yo hot headed ass either. This shit has always worked because our moves are calculated. The shit you on is bullshit, Juan."

"Stupid? They got fucking Griselda! That's the only blood in this world I got! Hell yeah I'll get stupid and knock a nigga block about her. That's your sister too hoe ass nigga!"

"Damn right that's my sister, but G is innocent. You acting like she's guilty of something. Our shit is clean. Think about it, nigga. They don't know us, our names, or nothing. All we gotta do is get her out and get with Vlad."

Denise came back in the room. "I talked to the Jews. They are on their way to get G. He looked in the system and she hasn't been arrested. He said that they popped Nadia Gomez during a drug ring and G was in the vicinity."

"That's good though cause it sounds like they hadn't made the drop yet so there are no drugs they can pen on G."

"Bro, we out of some muthafuckin bread. I sent the drop with fifty bands. Shit was supposed to double."

Denise was always the voice of reason, "Look, the most important thing is we are clean. We have the businesses and there's equity there in case of a rainy day. Juan, how much is in the emergency fund?"

"Two-Hundred."

"We can shake back with that for sure. See what Vlad talking about, Uno."

Juan grabbed his phone and walked out of the room, "I'm on it now!"

Tensions were high with everybody. Juan was scared for my safety and worried about getting popped. Ken was starting to get sick of Juan's erratic behavior, which was becoming a problem. Two weeks prior he had beat a nigga with a bottle in the club because he felt disrespected. Denise was scared for us all. She wanted her husband out of the game and now, more than ever, she wanted out of Houston. Although she never said it, we all knew that she despised Kenyon and Juan's relationship. She felt that he was going to bring Kenyon down. Regardless of the ill feelings, the time wasn't right for the bullshit. They had to come together to get me out and to make sure we didn't get busted. The reality was if they had one of us, they could've gotten us all.

While they were fussing and trying to figure shit out, I was stuck. The holding cell was cold. It was dark and it was filled with mold. I laid there thinking about how people spent their lives in jail. It damn near was inhumane. The cells were like animal cages. I can't front, that shit fucked up my mental. I wanted nothing more than to be released. I was having flashbacks of Mari and Marcus. I was going crazy, but I tried my best to control my emotions.

"Lynn, you're free to go," the guard yelled opening the door damn near four hours later.

I ran out of that muthafucka so quick I almost tripped. When I got to the lobby, I was greeted by someone that looked like Vlad. I knew he wasn't white and wasn't there to play any games based on his demeanor. He extended his hand, "Morano, nice to meet you."

"Hi," I responded still skeptical.

"Your family hired me to come and get you."

"My family," I questioned to see if he knew our code word. That would let me know if he had been sent by Juan.

"Mamita Uno," he responded extending his hand to open the door. When we exited the police station, there was a black Lincoln parked in front. Morano signaled for me to get in the back. He opened the door and to my surprise, Vlad was sitting in the back.

"Get in, dear," he greeted me with a smile.

I had this blank look on my face, confused as hell about him picking me up. He sensed my apprehension, "No worries. Uno called me to come and get you. Everything is going to be alright. There is a car waiting for you at my place. You can drive that back to Texas."

I nodded, "Thanks!"

"No, thank you, young lady, for being smarter than the average runner. Your silence saved us all. There will be rewards for your loyalty."

I didn't know what Vlad meant, but at that moment I didn't give a fuck. I just wanted to be back home with Mari. That stint in jail was enough for me to see that the dope game wasn't gone cut it and I needed to make sure my brother knew I was ready to get the fuck out.

Twenty-Five.

"What are you still doing woke, Kenyon?" Denise questioned.

"Can't sleep," he responded as he sat in their bedroom lounge chair.

Denise got up and went and sat on his lap, "Do you want to talk about it?"

"I'm ready to get out the game, Dee. We've been doing this shit for a while now. Once these businesses get up and running, I'm thinking about getting the fuck out. I just don't know about Juan."

"What about Juan?"

"That's my brother. When I had nobody else, I've always had him. Feel me? I don't want to leave him out there by himself. You know how foul these niggas be, Bae. That's my round."

"Kenyon, Juan is family and always will be. However! You don't owe him shit. At the end of the day you owe it to yourself and your family to get out. You can't sell drugs forever. For real, y'all have been lucky to not have anything really bad happen. I feel like God was sending a warning with G going to jail."

Kenyon shook his head, "I thought about that shit too. I ain't gone even lie."

"G told me this morning that she's ready to get out herself. What's crazy is y'all are both worried about the same thing; Juan's ass. Just because he has devoted his life to the game doesn't mean ya'll have to do the same, Kenyon. It's time for us to move the fuck on."

"I feel you, wife. I promise it won't be too much longer. My goal is to make sure shit sweet once we do break out. We can't be struggling with two kids."

"Speaking of the kids, Nina's mother called today to talk to Amire. I gave her the phone and I heard the bitch ask her if I was hitting her. They get on my nerves with that bullshit, Kenyon. For real."

"Don't worry about that, Dee. We got bigger fish to fry. If she can't be respectful she just can't talk to her no more. I ain't playing no games with them motherfuckers! Her old ass already told the cops she thought I had Nina killed. Scandalous ass! Bitch got all that insurance money and ain't do shit for Amire."

Denise hopped up, "You better get the old bitch before I do."

She rolled her neck as she threw her ass. Dee could be very sassy. Kenyon's eyes were deadlocked on her ass as it bounced. Dee had a southern body for real. Her skin was dark like a Godiva bar. She resembled her grandmother with her green eyes and sandy, brown hair. She stood about five four. Her build was solid and she had an ass shaped like an apple. It was thick, round and it bounced when she walked. Denise was really classy, but she always wore shit to show off her figure. Especially since she lost weight from the shooting. Kenyon loved her body, which made their sex life crazy.

"Get on the bed," he demanded.

Denise slid out of her silk nightgown and started crawling slowly across the bed. As she crawled her ass bounced and she looked over her shoulder seductively to entice Kenyon. He ripped off his boxers and stood facing the bed. Seven inches of hard dick dangled as he leaped on top of Denise. He kissed her neck and played with her pussy at the same time.

"Ahhh..." she moaned as he played with her clit.

She wrapped her hands around his head as he sucked her titties. He loved biting her nipples. Kenyon fingering her pussy while he gnawed on her nipples kept Denise fully aroused. Her pussy juices dripped as he slid his face between her legs. He spat on her pussy then slurped it all back up. The entire time Denise squirmed and moaned. Kenyon slid his hard dick into her pussy with a long stroke, "You like that?" he asked.

Denise was damn near speechless. She nodded in confirmation while biting her bottom lip.

"Damn," she screamed as Kenyon continued to stroke her long and hard. Her body began to shake as she started to cum. Cum shot onto his dick as she reached her climax.

"I'm bout to put a baby in you," Kenyon screamed as he nutted in Denise. He grabbed her body and held her close while he finished. Both of them were covered in sweat.

Kenyon looked into Denise's eyes as sweat dripped down his face, "I love you so fucking much, woman."

She could see the passion in his eyes and responded, "I love you more, husband."

They ended their night with a passionate kiss.

Twenty-Six.

"Right this way, Ms. Gonzales," the nurse instructed.

With everything that had been going on, I decided to go get checked out at the doctor. There was a rumor going around Sunnyside that Ryan had herpes. I knew I'd never get Marcus back unless he knew my shit was clean.

After the exam I waited in the room for my results. They had to send some of the tests to the lab, but some they gave me right away. My HIV test was negative, but I did have a yeast infection. Shit I felt like a weight was lifted off of my chest.

Soon as I left the office, I headed to Sunnyside to show Marcus my results. I actually found him hanging out at our shop.

"Good Morning," I stated as I walked in. We had hired a few workers and things were going well businesswise.

"What's good, G?" Marcus asked. He was in the back making himself a smoothie.

"I have to do some studying, can you make me a drink too?"

Marcus looked at me, "I got you. What's with the fuckin smile this morning?"

"I just came from the doctor," I handed him my results.

"This a good look for you!"

"That's all you have to say, Marcus?" I asked now irritated.

"I mean I'm glad you're straight. What you want me to say?"

I snapped, "You said that before we had sex you wanted me to get tested. There are the fuckin results."

Marcus sat down at the table, "G, we have a good thing going here. I don't want to ruin it with our personal drama. We co-exist in the shop cool and it has to stay that way."

"Bullshit! I know you. What happened that now you flexing on me? It wasn't an issue when I sucked your dick last night."

"Bianca don't want to have an abortion. I've been trying to convince her since I found out and she ain't been on the shit. Now, it's too late. She's having a little boy."

I couldn't believe it. Here I was planning our happily ever after and this bitch was trying to ruin it with this baby. It had been months since I even fucked with a nigga. I cut Ryan off right after the wedding. Marcus refused to fuck me so I was just giving him head here and there.

"Marcus, I still want to be back together, regardless if she has this baby or not. I'm not saying it won't be hard, but I at least want to try."

I caught him off guard. The look on his face was priceless. "G, what are you saying?"

"We both have done things in our relationship. It's my fault you even started fucking with Bianca. I don't like it, but as long as you don't love her I still want to work it out."

"So, you're telling me you can deal with me having another baby?"

I shook my head, "If you're willing to forgive me for cheating, we can make it through whatever."

Marcus didn't usually show affection in the shop, but when he stood up he smacked my ass and kissed me on the lips.

Although he didn't say it out his mouth, I knew that we were going to work it out. I knew that baby mama shit was gone be challenging so I needed to get some game from Dee. She had been raising Amire and things were going great for them.

Almost an hour later I had arrived at Dee's condo. When I walked in I could hear the music blasting loud as hell.

"Hey sis," Dee said as she welcomed me into the kitchen.

"It smells good in here, chica. ¿Que pasa conla comida?"

Dee laughed, "Don't come in here with all that Spanish shit nobody understands. I'm frying some chicken and making some greens for Ken."

"I definitely need parts of one of them plates yo."

"G, you're more than welcome. I know you ain't here about my cooking so what's going on?"

"I really need to talk to you about some shit."

Dee poured us both a glass of wine as I spilled out my guts.

I sighed, "Marcus told me this morning at the shop that Bianca decided to keep her baby. When he told me she was pregnant, he said that she was having an abortion. Now the bitch keeping the damn child."

"You already know how I feel about shit like that, honey. What you gone do?" Dee questioned.

"I mean I told Marcus that I was gone be there regardless. Shit, I want to be with him still. I don't know if I have any other choice."

"Griselda, you always have a choice! Now what you did with Ryan was fucked up, but you don't have to pay forever. You're still young. If this is not what you want, you don't have to settle for it. There's a lot of drama with that side bitch/baby mama shit. Make sure that's something you can handle. You also have to be willing to love the child as your own."

"Do you love Amire?"

"I do," Dee responded. "Now don't get it twisted her life almost cost me mines. For a long time that was a hard pill to swallow. I don't know if I'd still be with Kenyon if Nina was alive."

"So you think I should kill Bianca?"

Denise laughed, "No fool, but you really need to figure out if you can handle all of what this situation brings. Seriously! Marcus is young, G. We all settled down really early. Because of that there are going to be a lot of bumps with people learning to be adults."

"I really feel like we've had to teach ourselves you know? I'm not even twenty-one and both of my parents are dead. That's crazy to me."

"That is tough, but you're doing good. You have a few more months left of school. You own a business with the man you love. Sometimes you have to analyze all that you have opposed to all that you don't."

"I never thought about that. Damn!"

"Its real! That's why I told Kenyon it's time for us to move forward in our lives. Last week we decided that we are moving to Atlanta. I'm in the process of getting my license transferred to Georgia as we speak."

I damn near cried. Denise was really the only female in this world I had. I did not want to be without her. "Have ya'll told Juan? He's going to flip without Kenyon."

"Ken said he mentioned it to him, but I don't know how far it went. Juan is always in Atlanta so I'm sure they will be fine. As a woman I have to do what's best for my family you know?"

As much as I would have liked to be happy for Denise and Kenyon, I wasn't. It felt like I was losing them and that was going to be something I needed to grasp.

"I understand Dee. I'm just gone be so lost without you."

"No matter where I am G, you'll always have me. Family is forever and distance does not change that. Plus, you can always move to Georgia when you're ready!"

"Let Marcus and Juan start their bullshit. I'll be gone quick. ¡Rapidamente!"

Twenty-Seven

I hadn't been on the road since I was arrested. Juan felt that it would be best for me to chill for a while. Honestly, I didn't really mind. I was able to finish all my points for school and I had Mari everyday. Marcus still had a few credits to get, but he was almost finished.

Juan hosted a dinner for us to celebrate finishing school. Mamita's had opened in Atlanta so that's where he hosted it. We didn't have much family so it pretty much was the five of us, besides Dee's sister Rochelle. To all of our surprise, she had started dating Juan.

After we ate dinner, Dee stood up to give a speech. "First of all I want to say how much I love you all. As a family, we've come a long way. It's a blessing to be able to celebrate our babies tonight. Yes, Marcus and G, y'all are our babies dammit! No seriously I am really proud of y'all and there's nothing but success in the future for you both."

"My shit ain't gone be as nice as Dee's," Juan joked. "Naw, but on some real shit I'm happy as fuck. Ain't nothing more special than seeing my baby shine. Everything I do is for you and Mari. I love y'all more than I love money and everybody know I love fucking money. ¡Nene eres mi mundo!"

Kenyon interrupted, "Don't start that bullshit Juan. We all need to be able to understand you."

We all laughed. They always made fun of us when we spoke Spanish.

"Thank y'all! We definitely appreciate it. And y'all know we couldn't have made it this far without ya'll. I thank God for all of y'all. Real shit. We lost our parents and God made sure we weren't left without family."

"Already," Marcus replied.

"Enough of this mushy shit though, we've got business to discuss." Juan's words immediately changed the mood.

"What are you talking about," I asked.

"It's time to get back out here."

I was pissed. "So you mean to tell me that you want to talk about this shit right now? Here? At our graduation dinner?"

"Why not? We all here together."

Kenyon tried to intercept. "Uno, let's talk about this shit tomorrow, bro. We gone just enjoy the night."

"Fuck that! We need to talk about this shit now. Time waits for no man."

Rochelle grabbed Juan's arm to calm him down because he was pounding on the table.

"It's okay Rochelle, Juan what do you want to talk about?" I asked in a really low tone. It was apparent that my feelings were hurt.

"We bout to take shit to another level! Vlad got us connected with some dealerships and shit. All the product gone start coming on the trucks with the whips. The businesses legit! Our only move is to get the shit once it touch down."

Juan was so excited telling us about the new drug plan. No one else seemed interested. Dee rolled her eyes as he rambled on and Kenyon sat in silence. I don't think Marcus or Rochelle knew how to respond.

As much as I wanted to act like I wasn't bothered I couldn't. "Juan, why couldn't this wait?"

"What the fuck are you talking about, G?" he snapped.

"Nobody wants to talk about drugs all the fucking time!"

"You don't mind spending the drug money though do you?"

I stood up, "The money is not the problem- you are. All you care about is fucking dope and money. You don't care who gets hurt in the process. For one night I would've liked to have fun with my people and not discuss any bullshit. You couldn't even do that for me! We're all here dressed up and ready to kick it. But no. You always gotta ruin shit. I'm over this shit."

"Calm down, G," Marcus stated trying to break the tension.

"No, fuck that! He's selfish and I am sick of it," I yelled.

"Selfish!!!!!! My whole life I been grinding to make sure you were straight. Shit, all of ya'll for that matter. You sound real stupid and ungrateful, Grace."

"You just don't get it, Juan. Marcus, let's go!" I grabbed my purse and left the table. As much as I enjoyed the luxuries that came from having a Kingpin for a brother, I missed the normal shit. Juan was so out of touch with reality and that scared me. Hell, I didn't know if he even realized how emotionless he had become.

Twenty-Eight.

"Hey Stinky," Dee joked with her sister Rochelle.

"Don't start, Dee. I really need to talk to you about Juan."

Denise smirked her lips, "What's wrong with his crazy ass now?"

"I don't really think he like me."

"What are you talking about?"

Rochelle hesitated, "Our sex life is trash. His dick don't even stay hard."

"That don't surprise me, Ro. He ain't never got a woman. We've all been with somebody. Shit. You're the first girl I've known him to have."

"I don't know if I want to be with Juan. Something ain't right about him and his temper is mad crazy."

Dee replied, "Juan is a handful and you know his ass gets on my last nerve, but he's also security for you. Let that nigga take care of you while you finish school. Play your position. Start getting porn and doing freaky shit and see if that helps. But Ken just walked in, I'll have to talk to you later."

"Bye Bitch," Rochelle hung up the phone.

"Tell that nigga on the phone daddy's home," Kenyon joked.

Denise laughed, "Shut your ass up, fool. Don't nobody want me but you!"

"What's up though? You said we had something important to talk about. We going to Memphis tomorrow so I figured we'd chop it up today."

"What are you going to Memphis for?"

"I told you we're setting up shop in a new hood. Juan sending Marcus and Tone up there for a minute to get shit moving."

Dee became agitated, "So you mean to tell me he's leaving Marcus there by his lonely and you're okay with that?"

"Yeah! Why not? Marcus been keeping shit flowing down this bitch. If anybody can set shit up its him."

"For somebody that's supposed to be getting out. Your ass sho in the mix! I don't like that shit and I don't want you leaving Marcus in no got damn Memphis, Kenyon."

Kenyon wasn't trying to hear what Dee had to say. "Look, let me handle this shit and you worry about something else. I know you didn't call me home to bitch about the moves I'm making for us."

"We agreed that you'd get out, Kenyon. It's almost a new year and I am ready to leave Texas."

"It's going to happen, Dee. Damn! Stop rushing the shit. When it's time for us to shake, we will! I can't be under all this fucking pressure when I come home. It's fucked up enough in the streets."

"Kenyon, I can't lose you!!! What the fuck I'm gone do if you get caught or, God forbid, worse. What yo three kids gone do? At the end of the day, I'm looking out for you."

Kenyon paused for a second. "What you mean three kids?"

"I'm pregnant."

"What? When you find out?" he asked still in shock.

"This morning that's why I had you come home so we could talk about everything."

"Damn! This ain't the time for another kid!"

Denise became infuriated, "Kenyon, we had KJ when we were sixteen! Now, we are married and got our shit together. Why wouldn't this be a good time?"

"Bae, I ain't mean it like that. We're just trying to move, get these businesses off the ground and it's a lot going on that's all."

"Fuck you Kenyon; you think I'm stupid. Your ass just ain't ready to leave this bullshit behind. I tell you what- by the New Year your ass better be ready to go to Georgia. Otherwise, plan on being a single ass nigga with your daughter."

Twenty-Nine.

Juan and I hadn't really been talking since my graduation dinner, but we had unfinished business. The first shipment had come in off the trucks and we had to get the dope to Memphis. At first I wasn't gone do it, but to my surprise, Marcus talked me into it.

When I arrived at the warehouse, Marcus was inside with Kenyon and Juan. I walked in greeting everyone but Juan.

"¿Que pasa?" he asked. I knew he was trying to break the ice by speaking in Spanish. When we were little, Papi used to wake us up in the morning screaming, "¿Que pasa?" like a comedian.

"Mierda," I replied sarcastically.

"What's good baby sis?" Kenyon interrupted.

"Nothing much! How was my baby last night?"

Marcus joked, "Now you know this nigga don't have a clue. They asses been at the casino for damn near two days."

"Conseguir mucho dinero," Juan said rubbing his hands together.

"That's a damn shame. Dee gone kick yo ass, Ken. Don't let Uno get you in trouble."

Ken shook his head, "You ain't never lied, G. But anyway did Uno tell you the plan?"

"Nope! That's why I'm here now."

"We need you to transport three keys of boy to Memphis."

"Hold up! Marcus, you said I'd just have to take pills."

"I know Bae but Rochelle backed out on us," he replied.

"This is bullshit. I told ya'll I wasn't feeling this driving shit no more!"

Juan caught an attitude, "Look Grace you're all we got. Muthafuckin family sticks together and we need you. I promise everything will be smooth. You don't even have to drive the shit."

"What are you talking about," I questioned.

"You're going to ride the Greyhound bus. There are no metal detectors or any security. You can get on the bus with an overnight bag. The dope will be taped to your body and sealed to control the smell."

"You niggas are out of ya'll fuckin minds!"

Kenyon, always being the voice of reason, pleaded with me. "G, this is actually safer than you driving. All you have to do is catch the bus. It's a long ride but you have nothing to worry about. Grab a book or some shit and just rock out. When you get there, Marcus will pick you up from the bus station. He'll already be there."

"Marcus, you didn't tell me you were going too."

"Bae, I'll be up there for a little minute setting up shop. Juan and Ken will be back and forth."

"Why do you have to stay up there alone?"

"Don't trip. Lil Tone gone be up there with me. I'll be straight and once shit moving smoothly, I'm coming home. I promise."

"Whatever," I responded annoyed with the entire situation. Marcus and I had been doing really well and I trusted his judgment. I wasn't feeling my brother, but I knew he had my back. So, I agreed and caught the bus two days later with three kilos of boy. Dee told me not to do it, but my loyalty wouldn't let me do otherwise.

Thirty

"Aye Tone, get the door, nigga!" Marcus yelled.

Tone got up and went to the door, but no one was there. "Marc, you hearing shit. Ain't nobody at this damn door."

"On life I heard somebody knock. Oh well, fuck it. We gotta hit the basement and bag this shit up."

Marcus headed downstairs with the drugs to cut and bag it up. Tone shut the house down as they normally did and headed for the basement.

"Aye bro, we gotta get some lights around this bitch. It's dark as fuck round' here."

Marcus schooled Tone, "That's how we want it when we handling our shit. Niggas don't need to know whether we here or not. Plus, shit we from Sunnyside. These Memphis niggas cut from a different cloth."

"You ain't never lied about that shit bro. I had to go off on the little nigga Jeezy the other day. This nigga was trying to flex in front of his bitch at the store," Tone explained.

"That's why we gotta lay low and stay out these niggas' way. Don't get it twisted though. Uno got shit on smash and will get shit poppin if need be!"

Tone laughed, "That nigga nuts man. I remember when he split Peanut head cause he said Grace looked like she had some good pussy."

"He should have. Fuck Peanut! His hoe ass always got something to say about my bitch."

"Nigga she done had you on lock for a grip. She is bad though."

Marcus grinned, "I love that stupid ass girl. Bianca just got my shit all fucked up with this fucking baby. I started to off her muthafuckin ass for real."

"Shit, I'll do it for the right price," Tone started using his hands to mimic a gun.

"You a wild boy man. We ain't catching no bodies, nigga. We getting money. That's what we on. We got killers for that other shit, but finish up here. I'm bout to go grab some wings from Lil' Tia spot."

"Make sure you grab me a plate too, I'm hungry as fuck," Tone replied continuing to bag the drugs.

Once Marcus was gone, Tone picked up his burner to make a call. "Aye, shit in rotation. Make sure you where you supposed to be when you're supposed to be. Shit bout to get real."

Marcus spent a few hours over Lil' Tia's house. She was a hoodrat that he met fucking around in Memphis. He would go have sex with her and get a home cooked meal from time to time. It was nothing serious. She was just something to occupy his time while they were in Memphis.

When Marcus arrived back at the spot, he noticed it was still dark. He mumbled, "Why the fuck this nigga ain't back up and running."

As he unlocked the door, he was pulled in by two men in all black.

Pow! Marcus was struck in the face by one of the men holding a pistol. Blood splattered from his nose and mouth. The same man with the gun demanded that Marcus unlock the safe. Ironically, the man knew exactly where it was. Unable to see clearly, Marcus stumbled to where the safe was located inside of the furnace.

"Bitch nigga, who the man now?" the other guy taunted while cracking Marcus in the back of the head with his gun.

Marcus pleaded, "Look, y'all can have it all. Just don't kill me!"

Once the safe was finally open, the men pushed Marcus out of the way and put everything inside into a backpack.

"Yo, this ain't shit! Where the rest of the money nigga!" The guy removed his mask and there Tone was standing over Marcus with a 40 aimed at his head.

Despite his vision being distorted, Marcus recognized Tone. He couldn't speak but his heart was shattered. He had brought Tone in the mix. Marcus remembered how Kenyon got him out of a bad situation and he wanted to do the same for another little nigga. This time his loyalty backfired and his life was on the line.

Part Four

Thirty-One

"Kenyon Green please," the lady on the phone asked.

Dee was furious, "Kenyon is married. Who the fuck is this?"

"I do apologize for calling so late. My name is Anna Mason. I am a nurse at Methodist North Hospital."

"Methodist North Hospital," Dee questioned.

"Yes. Mr. Green's number was found on a victim of a shooting. We believe they are related."

Dee's heart sunk, "Who is the victim?"

"Marcus Murray!" As the nurse spoke, Denise zoned out of it. She immediately began screaming, which woke up everyone in the house.

Kenyon rushed into their bedroom, "Yo, what the fuck is going on?"

When he walked in the room he found Denise laid out across their bedroom floor in shambles.

Kenyon panicked, "Denise, baby what's wrong?" he asked picking her up off the ground.

"Baby, it's Marcus somebody shot him in Memphis."

Dee sobbed and Kenyon sat there on the floor in a daze. He heard Denise but he could not emotionally process what she said. After a few minutes, he probed again. "Denise, what do you mean Marcus got shot?"

She handed him the phone, "Call that number back."

"Methodist North Hospital," a lady answered.

"My name is Kenyon Green. I am calling regarding to my brother Marcus Murray."

"One moment please," she responded. Within a few seconds, a man took over the call.

"This is Detective McGuire."

"What's going on Detective?" Kenyon asked nervously.

"Mr. Green, your number was found in Mr. Murray's jacket pocket. It had bro written on it so I am assuming you guys are related correct?"

"Yeah, that's my God-brother," Kenyon responded.

"I think it would be best if your family came into the hospital so we could speak to you guys in more detail, if that's okay?"

Kenyon asked the detective if Marcus was dead. He refused to provide him with an answer, instead he advised him to get there as soon as he could.

"Fuck!" Kenyon yelled. "Bae, call Uno and get him over here. We gotta get to Memphis."

Within an hour both Juan and I had arrived at Ken and Dee's house.

"Yo, this shit better be good! Ya'll muthafuckas waking me up out my sleep. It better be some money involved," Juan yelled.

"Uno, shut yo ass up please," Dee asked in a gentle tone.

I started to notice their demeanors and I knew something was wrong. "What's going on ya'll?"

"G, they called from Memphis. Marcus got shot."

"What?" Juan asked standing up out of the chair.

"Bro we don't know shit else. They found my number in his jacket. Some nurse and detective with him. The nigga said we need to get there ASAP!"

"Oh my God," I yelled as my body started to quiver.

Dee wrapped her arms around my shoulders. "Its okay G, we just gotta get up there and see what the fuck is going on."

"Ken, ditch that number bro! Where is that nigga Tone?" Juan was furious.

"I don't know. They didn't mention shit about dude and his burner done. I called like fifty times."

Juan started to pound on the table, "We gotta get to Memphis! Dee, I need you to find us some flights. G, go home and secure shit. I'll meet ya'll at the warehouse in bout an hour. Don't be late we gotta get up the way."

We all nodded and moved sluggishly trying to get ourselves together. Marcus needed us and like always, it was family first.

Thirty-Two

"So what's the word Bro?" Kenyon questioned.

"Man, I don't know shit. Marcus left to go eat at some little bitch spot. Shit, while he was gone I ducked off into some pussy. I got back and the crib was surrounded so I bounced," Tone responded.

Juan sat in silence listening to his story.

Kenyon yelled, "Nigga, why you ain't call us?"

"My phone was in the spot and shit I knew the burner was bad. Closest spot I knew to go to was the little bitch Marc was fucking with. She told me he had left to go home. I didn't know what the fuck to do…DAMN, THEY GOT MY NIGGA."

"This shit is crazy mane. All the moves we done made and my nigga get smoked up this bitch! Somebody know something and I ain't leaving Memphis til I get to the bottom of this shit and that's on my kids."

Juan finally spoke, "Tone, ya'll ain't have no problems with nobody around here? No niggas or bitches?"

"Naw Big Bro. It was some little niggas hatin' but nothing too serious. I don't know what the fuck this shit was about for real for real."

Juan nodded, "Ight, I'm gone check out the city and see what's up. We gotta meet G and Dee at the hospital and shit. The spot is shut down though. Don't go back to that bitch. For real it's time for you to head back to Sunnyside too, just to make sure you ain't in danger."

"Man, I don't even want to go back without my nigga. Shit just ain't the same. I was thinking about going to Cali with my people man for a little minute."

"Word?" Kenyon questioned.

"Hell yeah this shit too much for a nigga to take. What I do know though is, when we find these hoe ass niggas, I ain't shedding no mercy on em'."

"Mercy is for Dios, I came to bring pain," Juan stated as he headed out of the hotel eatery.

Kenyon and Juan got into a rental and Tone headed off in an unmarked car. Neither Juan nor Kenyon spoke the entire ride to the hospital. They were numb and wanted blood.

When they finally arrived at the hospital, Dee and I were already done talking to the detectives.

"Dee, what they say?" Juan asked.

"Basically, it was a robbery and they believe that it was drug related. The lady detective said they received an anonymous call a few days before saying that drug were being sold out of the house."

"Anonymous huh?" Juan responded rubbing his hands across my back.

I tried to keep it together as long as I could, but I just couldn't. I broke down at the hospital. Juan and Kenyon consoled me. Death had stolen my parents and now Marcus. For the life of me I couldn't figure out why it was happening to us again. My heart was crushed and I did not know how I was going to explain to Mari that her daddy was gone.

Thirty-Three.

It took damn near two weeks for us to get Marcus's body back to Texas. The detectives in Memphis kept it until they finished their investigation. Basically, they ain't find shit. There were no drugs in the crib, no dna or fingerprints; nothing. All they had was Marcus's blood. We weren't okay with that shit either! Bottom line, I needed answers. A few days before the services, I sat everybody down.

"¿Hermana, que pasa?" Juan asked.

"I've been all over the place since all this shit happened ya'll. I keep praying asking Mary to reveal to me what the fuck happened to Marcus. After talking to that nigga Tone, something ain't right. I think they set Marcus up."

"That nigga won't return none of my calls. I let his people know the funeral was in a few days. He better be there," Kenyon added.

Dee had her hands over her mouth. I knew we were on the same page. "The detectives said there were no signs of forced entry or nothing. Shit, they didn't even take his jewelry or nothing else."

As we all theorized, Juan remained silent the entire conversation.

"I did get a hold of Alexis and his brothers. They want answers just like we do. I think we should hire a private investigator. Them crackers don't give a fuck about our lives. They think he was a bad person so they are not going to investigate this shit right yall."

Finally, Juan decided to speak. "Look, G, all I need you to worry about is Mari and getting through this funeral shit. We'll handle the rest. I promise on Mamita and Papi we're going to find these putas!"

"Hell yeah. Niggas gotta pay for this one. Period! G, don't talk to nobody else about this shit. If somebody comes and brings info to you let me know. We out here on it though."

Juan stood up, "I'm gone take you and Pookie out to dinner tonight. Dee, I love you sis thank you for everything. Ken, my nigga meet me at the spot in like thirty."

After Juan and Ken left the shop, Dee and I stayed talking.

"G, how you holding up?"

I could barely process my thoughts. "I'm really just fucked up Dee. Thank God Candace been staying at the house with me."

"I know…it's fucking me up too. I just feel so bad because Marcus has always been like our son. I'm actually pissed at Juan and Ken for leaving him up there by himself. It's all just so fuckin crazy!"

"I feel the same. Now is just not the time to bust their fucking bubble. I tell you what though once this shit is over we're out of here. If you and Ken still moving, we're coming with ya'll. I don't give up a fuck about the shop or the houses. I'm done with Texas and all this drug bullshit flat out," I screamed.

Dee clapped her hands together. "Yup! It's time baby sis. I told Kenyon that shit too. We the fuck out of here. Him and Juan better start getting their shit together cause this life ain't a forever type of deal. Fuck that! We have kids involved."

"You're right, Dee!"

"G, once we get Marcus to rest we can get busy on getting the fuck out of here. I promise I got you sis. I'll never leave you and Mari out here for dead. This family shit we got is forever, even if I have to leave Kenyon's ass. As long as I'm alive you'll never be alone."

We stood in the middle of the shop crying and hugging each other. With both of my parents being gone and Marcus, I thanked God for Dee. She was always there for us, even when she was sick of Juan's shit. I didn't know how I was necessarily going to make it through, but at least I had somebody to go through it with me.

Once Dee was gone, somebody started knocking on the shop's door. I opened it and Bianca was standing there.

"What do you want?" I asked.

"I want to talk about Marcus's funeral, Griselda. My son's name should be included in the obituary."

I immediately got heated. "Bitch, first of all we don't know if that's even Marcus's son. The baby like a fucking week old. Get out of here with that bullshit, Bianca."

"You just mad cause I have a child by Marcus that's all. Yo mad ass ain't gone change my son's DNA. Whether you like it or not Mari and Marcus are brother and sister."

I approached Bianca who was standing by the door. "You rat faced bitch I don't give a fuck about shit you talking about. At the end of the day we both know where Marcus's heart was. With me like its always been. Yo muthafuckin son ain't going in shit and I dare you to try something at this funeral. I will muthafuckin end you!"

Bianca responded, "I tried to come to you like a real woman, but obviously you still on that bullshit. Marcus is dead neither one of us can have him. Yea, you was his main bitch you got that. So what? That don't change what we had. He loved you, but that don't mean that he didn't love me too. You could never end that."

"Get yo raggedy, broke ass out OUR muthafuckin shop hoe before I drag you out. The only child that's gone be in his obituary is Mari Murray. Period, point, blank!"

Bianca didn't say another word. Instead she turned around and walked out of the shop. I couldn't stand that bitch and it took everything in me not to beat her ass. The truth was her son could've very well been Marcus's baby. We planned on getting a paternity test once he was born. I didn't give a fuck though. My heart couldn't take the shit when he was alive and I damn sure couldn't take it with him being gone. I had to hold on to every good thing I could about the man that I loved. Shit, sharing him with some bitch and her baby was out of the muthafuckin question.

Thirty-Four.

Everybody met up at the shop in Sunnyside before going to the funeral home. I was still in shock that we were actually burying Marcus.

"How you holding up," Alexis asked. It was crazy because we barely saw her. Even Marcus couldn't tell you where she lived. Their relationship was always fucked up, but I was happy she was there. He was her son.

"This is a lot Lex. I don't even really know how to feel."

She grabbed Mari out of the chair. Juan bought her a Versace dress with some matching slippers. Her hair was braided into two ponytails; she was fly. "If my grandbaby ain't the sharpest thing in the room honey!"

We both laughed. As we were giggling Marcus's brothers walked up. It had been years since we seen AJ, Shawn and Marvin. Alexis was so wild that they ended up getting separated when they were younger. Kenyon took in Marcus and the boys ended up with their father's families. I was so happy to see them. We just hugged and of course Alexis started crying.

"Can everybody gather around for prayer please?" Dee interrupted the chatter.

She hired her mother's pastor to do the eulogy and he was there to do the prayer as well. I wasn't on it. I was mad at God and couldn't accept that "his will be done" shit.

Kenyon and Juan grabbed my hands and escorted me to the family car once the prayer was over. I laid my head on Juan's chest as we rode, trying to forget I was going to bury the love of my life.

"Hello," Kenyon answered his phone.

"Who dat?" Juan interrupted.

Kenyon ignored him, "Cool…!" He hung up quick.

"Nigga, who was on the phone?" Juan snapped

Kenyon was irritated, "Shut the fuck up, Uno. That info we needed from up the way came through. Chill out, nigga. It's that time."

"Already!"

I didn't know what they were talking about, but I had a feeling something was about to go down. Whatever it was I could see the difference in Kenyon's energy since he took the call. I think Dee was concerned as well.

"Bae, when we get to the church, I want you to escort Lex in. She's going to sit on the first row next to us. There's room for his brothers as well. Anybody else gotta sit on the second row, " Dee instructed.

Kissing her on the forehead he nodded in agreement.

When we arrived Juan walked in with Mari and I. All I can recall is walking in and going over to Marcus's casket. Soon as I saw him in the casket, I dropped to the floor screaming. That shit was horrific. I couldn't take it and had to be escorted to the back of the funeral home. Juan had Mari and I just needed to be alone to process everything. While I was gone, apparently some mess popped off in the chapel when Bianca showed up.

"Kenyon, can I talk to you?" Bianca asked.

"Sup B?" he responded.

She handed him the obituary. "Why they didn't put Little Marcus name in here, bro?"

"Yo, you already know what that shit about! Marcus didn't even know if the baby was his, B. Now ain't the time for that shit."

Bianca's mother butted in. "That's bullshit! My grandson looks just like Marcus. Kenyon, you know he was with my daughter. Y'all got all these pictures of that girl and her baby in this thing; y'all could've put him in here. That ain't right."

Juan walked up, "Oh y'all got a problem with my sister and my niece?"

Neither one of them responded.

"I said do we got a muthafuckin problem? Neither one of you bitches bet not say shit about my sister. Fuck out of here with this hoe shit yall on!" Juan was pissed.

"Come on Uno. We gotta get G before this shit start. Y'all might want to leave this shit alone before it turn into some other shit. B, I know you loved Marc, its just all around fucked up."

She nodded her head at Kenyon as he walked away with Juan. By the time they came and got me, Bianca and her mother were gone. God knows that was for the best because I was ready to catch a body, literally.

After the singers were done, they gave people some time to speak about Marcus. Kenyon spoke first, " When I think about Marcus, I can only smile. From day one he loved me. He wanted to do everything I did and go where I went. That was my brother. Blood couldn't make us any closer. There has not been one day that we haven't talked, laughed and cried together. My life will never be the same man. This kind of pain is just unbearable. I just want y'all to know I loved my brother with all my heart and I'm gone miss him."

Everybody clapped for Kenyon and then Alexis grabbed the microphone, "I remember the day I brought my baby home from the hospital. He was so little and filled with so much joy. Marcus had a good heart and he loved his family and friends. I thanked God for Kenyon and Juan because they became the father Marcus didn't have. No matter what we went through, I loved my son and I pray that God gets whoever did this. Please pray for my family and our peace as we try to make sense of all of this. My beautiful granddaughter lost her father. She needs us all."

Hearing Alexis speak about Mari losing her father really did something to me. I couldn't believe that he was gone. I was up next and could barely keep my composure. The crowd supported me as I tried to get myself together to speak. Finally, I caught my breath and as tears flowed from my eyes I spoke, "I don't really know what to say right now. My heart is shattered. Marcus and I have been together since we were kids. We've done everything together! I really don't know how I'm gone go on without him. I don't know what I'm going to tell my daughter. I'm angry! I want whoever did this to him to pay. I can't talk to God right now. So, y'all gone have to pray for me. To Marcus: I love you with all of my heart and always will. Rest easy my King."

Both Juan and Dee decided not to say anything. Shawn and AJ, Marcus's brothers, said a few nice words. They mentioned recently reconnecting with Marcus and being happy about their plans to get together. I knew Marcus really wished they were closer. Shawn let Mari and I know that he would always be there for us if we needed him. I appreciated that.

Once the services were over, we headed to the cemetery. When I tell you Sunnyside showed mad love, it was real. All the homies came out in the dunks. They had DSR's gangster lean blasting as we dropped him the ground. That's what I loved most about our hood. When shit got real, everybody came out. We all danced and sung along as we cried and dropped roses into the grave. Juan's crazy ass was standing on top of the car screaming, "Rest easy Marc Dawg!"

Thirty-Five

"What's up G?" Denise questioned.

"Nothing much Dee just laying here on this couch."

"Where is Mari? Did Lex come get her like she said?"

Marcus had been dead a month and I was really depressed. I wasn't doing anything but sleeping all day. Juan held down the operation and Ken made sure everything was straight at the shop. Since Marcus' funeral, his mother and brothers had stepped in and started helping with Mari. I was appreciative because I was really fucked up and didn't have much energy. Out of everybody though, Dee had been my rock.

"She came and got her. I was a little apprehensive but she said they were going to some resort with Shawn."

I heard Dee clapping, "That's good! Shit, it's definitely time that they stepped up."

"Hell yeah. It's quiet over there. Where Ken and the kids?"

"Girl, he's running the streets with Juan as usual. Both of the kids are with Mommy. She's keeping them for the weekend. That means that we can go out and hang a little bit."

I didn't want to leave the house. "Dee, I appreciate it but I just want to chill."

"No!" she yelled.

"What you mean no?" I questioned.

"Griselda, it's time for you to start picking up your pieces. I know your heart is broken, but Marcus would not want you to die with him. All I'm saying is: let's get some fresh air and have a cocktail. If you ain't feeling it, we can leave."

"Fuck it. Why not. You're driving though. I don't even think my damn whip got no gas in it."

Dee laughed, "Girl, we gotta get you together. That sounds fuckin crazy. Get dressed and I'll be there in like an hour. Don't be acting crazy either when you see the Range. That's all me."

"Let me find out you still got Kenyon tricking." We both laughed hanging up the phone. I knew Dee had my best interest at heart, that's why I got my ass up. Everything I had been through she was there. I wanted her to know that she was appreciated.

When Dee pulled up, I was shocked to see her whip. As long as we had been getting money, Ken and Dee remained modest. Well besides Dee and her bags. Ken also had a few nice whips and some designer clothes, but nothing too spectacular.

"Aye, this is lit!" I yelled opening up the door.

"Thank you Sis. It's a guilt gift from Kenyon."

"Guilt?" I questioned.

Dee turned down the music and we drove off, "Well, before Marcus passed, we found out I was pregnant. As happy as I was, Kenyon didn't feel the same. Shit between all the stress from the funeral and work and shit, I became overwhelmed. My husband barely comes home anymore. He's always with your fuckin' brother. My blood pressure got stupid a few weeks ago after arguing with him; I miscarried."

"¡Dios! Why didn't you call me, Dee?" I asked pissed that she didn't reach out.

"G, you have enough on your plate with Marcus and Mari. The last thing you need to be worried about is my shit. I am a grown, married woman. I can handle it."

"That's bullshit and you know it, Denise. We've always had each other's backs. Shit, you helped raise me. No matter what I'm going through, you're always there. I want to be there for you too sometimes."

"Aww G, I love you! I really appreciate that."

I smirked, "Whatever! Don't let it happen again or its gone be some shit. Anyway, where are we going?"

"It's called Hermanos. They got some bomb ass margaritas. Ken brought me here last week to have lunch."

When we pulled up, my anxiety kicked in. The place was an authentic Mexican spot that reminded me of Mamita and Papi. For some odd reason I couldn't help but long for them.

Dee noticed my silence, "You good, G?"

"Yeah, I'm straight. This spot just reminds me of mis padres."

"Yo dad? Shit, you know I don't know that Spanish shit, heifa."

I laughed, "It means my parents fool."

"Oh shit! That makes sense, but don't trip. Let's just go in here and try to enjoy ourselves. We need it."

When we walked in, we were greeted by two servers wearing large sombreros.

"Bienvenido a Hermanos," one of the waitresses stated.

"Gracias," I responded as they escorted us to our table.

Dee started joking as soon as we sat down. "See bitch, I gotta learn Spanish. Kenyon keep fucking up I'm gone have to roll up on me a Papi."

"Girl bye! You ain't leaving Kenyon's ass. Or he ain't letting you for that matter."

"G, let me explain something to you. Kenyon and I have been together since we were kids. When I was a young chick growing up, I didn't mind him being in the streets. Shit, he kept me fly and when KJ was born we wanted for nothing. However, as time goes on I want more. The dope game is no longer for me. I don't give a fuck about the money or none of that other shit. I want my husband out. Too much bullshit is starting to happen. First you went to jail, then Marcus dying. G, I don't feel good about this shit no more."

"It's crazy that you said that. On Mari, I been thinking bout this shit since Marcus died. Like I don't want to be involved at all anymore. Before I wasn't scared of shit. Even after going to jail I wasn't scared. Now, I'm terrified. I don't want to die nor do I want to lose anybody else. If something happened to Juan or Ken, I would die. The problem is my brother is in so deep. I feel like I can't leave him out there alone."

Our food had arrived. We continued talking as we ate quesadillas and sipped our margaritas.

Dee stirred her drink as she spoke, "G, both you and Kenyon have this loyalty to Juan that's gone be y'all downfall. Don't get it twisted, I love Juan like an annoying ass brother. He's family for sure, but he's selfish. His mind is so stuck on being Pablo Escobar, he can't see the danger in this shit anymore. Between the businesses and cash, we all have enough money to bow out and live decent until the next thing comes up. Ken ain't on it though because he don't want to leave Juan. Now, you on the same shit!"

"I don't want to be, Dee. I promise. I just don't know how to tell my brother. He depends on me to have his back. Our shit been solid for so long because we never let any outsiders in. If you ask me that's why Marcus is dead."

"I think so too, G. Not to mention the game has changed. Niggas full of jealousy and stay snitching."

"Girl, Marcus dying got us all fucked up. I don't even know where to begin to pick up the pieces. Honestly, I never saw any of this coming. I just wanted to get money and be with my family. All of this other shit is extra."

"G, as fucked up as it is, this all a part of the game. We always saw how niggas died and went to jail and shit. When you think about it though, we never really considered how the women in their lives were affected."

I marinated on what Dee had said. It was true. The dope game really ruined families. Growing up we always seen niggas dying and going to the joint. People really only seemed to care about the loss of those lives. Nobody ever seemed to care about the moms, baby moms and grandmas that were left to raise the kids alone.

"Damn, Dee, that's deep for real. I never really thought about that. Now look at us, all caught up in the shit and barely making it out."

"Cold world, dirty game," she responded as we both slipped into a daze. We were buzzed, full of pain and madder than a muthfucka.

Thirty-Six

"Hurry the fuck up, nigga. Taking all muthafuckin day," Juan yelled.

"Shut the fuck up, Uno. I got this nigga."

"This nigga gone be spooked when he see us, Ken."

Kenyon shook his head, "Hell yeah. He should've known he could only run from us for so long."

"Welp, you know what time it is."

After an hour and a half drive, Juan and Kenyon arrived at a warehouse in Memphis. Although they were together, they rode in silence. They didn't even speak once they reached their destination. They walked in and peeped the scene. Everything was set up properly. Juan went to the back of the building, while Ken locked the doors.

"She up?" Kenyon asked.

"The dumb bitch back there crying and shit."

"Oh, now she crying?" Kenyon asked sarcastically.

"You ready?" Juan asked looking into Ken's eyes for confirmation.

Ken rubbed his hands together, "On kids, I been waiting for this shit. I ain't never been more ready, nigga."

Juan started to walk to the back and Kenyon followed. There was a young lady tied up in a back room with tape around her mouth. Tears of terror flowed from her eyes as the men approached her.

Removing the tape from her mouth, Kenyon instructed her to sit up.

"PLEASE," she yelled before Juan told her to shut the fuck up.

"Look, I want to know what happened to my brother and I want the truth. You got one chance to tell your side of the story."

"I don't know what you're talking about," she lied.

Juan started to get irritated, "Let's just off this lying bitch, Bro. Hoe, we know you know what the fuck happened to Marcus. Stop with the bullshit before I splat yo shit!"

Kenyon put his hands up, cutting Juan off. "LaTia Janae Melrose, tell us what the fuck happened if you ever want to see your kids again."

After a few minutes of sitting in silence she finally was able to gain her composure and speak. "I was fucking around with Marcus. Him and Little Tone would come to my crib to eat and smoke sometime. Well one night Tone came by himself, well he wasn't with Marcus. He was with some other dude I didn't know. He said he was from down the way too. They told me that Marcus was trippin on his bitch from back home and needed some pussy. Tone gave me a couple yards and told me to get something special together and have Marc come through the next day. I didn't think much of it, I thought he was looking out for his nigga."

"So what you say to Marc?" Ken asked.

"I called him and asked him to come over. I had told him that I cooked something for us to eat and wanted to suck his dick."

"Bitch, how did you know when to call?" Juan yelled.

"Tone had called me from a private number a few hours before and told me when Marcus was gone be free," she responded.

Kenyon was furious, "What happened next?"

"He came over and we ate. We ended up having sex and he left afterwards. The next day I heard from a gettyup that he was shot at the spot." As she spoke tears flowed from her eyes.

"Did you know they were going to kill Marcus?" Kenyon asked firmly.

"On my kids I did not know what was going to happen. I promise you. I had no clue. Marcus was cool as fuck. I had love for him. I would've never did that shit to him."

Juan didn't believe her. "Well why you ain't call the police once you knew he got smoked?"

"Tone showed up to my house. He told me they were investigating Marcus's murder and since I was the last person he was with, not to say nothing. He gave me a few yards to get a new phone and said shit was about to get real. Some nigga named Uno was supposed to be coming from down the way to get whoever got Marcus. I was scared and didn't want no part of that. I got three kids to raise."

Once she was done talking, they taped her mouth again. Afterwards, they left the room.

"She dying too Ken! I'm smoking this dumb ass bitch. Ain't nothing she can say gone convince me she didn't know shit wasn't solid."

"Bro, we gone use this hoe to get that nigga back here."

Juan paused, "What you mean?"

"Tone gone fuck with this bitch to make sure she don't tell. He ain't too far, trust me. Any real nigga would've already killed her. She know too fuckin much. Instead this hoe ass nigga underestimating her and got her out here by her lonely."

"Nigga, you right!"

"Uno, I gotta go in by myself this time. She's scared of you. I bet she know how to get in contact with this nigga."

"I got her joint in the box," Juan replied.

"Did you turn the signal and shit off," Kenyon questioned nervously.

"Of course! I had Mike Mike disable the whole shit. Go look through that bitch for a number for this nigga. I bet it's in there."

Juan handed the phone to Kenyon and he went to confront Tia.

"Look, I don't want to hurt you Lil'Mama. You gone have to help me out though. Which one of these numbers in yo phone is Tone's?"

She hesitated and didn't speak for a few minutes. "He said to store him under Sunnyside."

Kenyon entered the number on the burner and dialed Tone's number. He put the phone to Tia's ear.

"Yo, Tee, what's good?"

Tia spoke nervously, "Tone, you in Memphis right now?"

"Yeah, I'm over your friend house. It's crazy you called me though I just got here."

Kenyon was instructing Tia on what to say.

"Oh okay, I want to get up with you while you're here."

"Everything okay?" Tone questioned.

"Yeah...a detective came to my crib though. Apparently a neighbor seen Marcus leaving my house."

Tone was silent for a few seconds. "Where you at?"

"I'm over my people's. We can meet up behind Mook's spot. Nobody will see us there. Don't tell Tierra that you talked to me either. I don't need nobody else to know."

"Bet! Give me about an hour and I'll be there."

"Okay," Tia responded.

"Don't trip babygirl everything gone be straight. See you in a few."

When the phone hung up, Kenyon went and told Juan what went down. They agreed that Juan would stay at the warehouse and Ken would go meet Tone. He had arrived early on the scene just to make sure shit was kosher. There weren't any cameras set up. It was pitch black and Tone was alone. Kenyon spotted Tone pacing nervously waiting for Tia to arrive. He crept up behind him, holding a 38 revolver to his back. A masked Kenyon instructed Tone to get in the trunk. He had already clipped the trunk's lever so he couldn't get out. About twenty minutes later, they arrived at the warehouse. This time Kenyon drove the car inside.

Thirty-Seven

Juan sat patiently at a desk inside of the warehouse. He was looking for commercial properties while he waited on Kenyon to arrive.

"Like butter baby," Kenyon stated as he hopped out of the car.

"That simple huh?" Juan joked.

Kenyon pointed to the backroom asking, "What we gone do about her?"

"It's already done! I told you that bitch knew too much, K."

There was a pause in Kenyon's movements. Despite wanting Tone's head, a part of him believed that Tia was telling the truth and he didn't want her to die.

Juan snapped at Kenyon's silence. "Fuck wrong with you nigga? Stop acting pussy and lets handle this fuck boy."

Tone heard Juan's voice from the inside of the trunk and pissed on himself. He knew what he did to Marcus was wrong, but he needed the money. Or at least that's how he justified it. Regardless of his reasoning, Tone crossed The Squad and would have to pay.

Juan dimmed the warehouse lights while Ken popped the trunk. They pulled Tone out and strapped him to a wooden chair. While Ken adjusted the straps around his ankles, Juan removed the cover from his face.

"Amigo," Juan smiled revealing his face to Tone.

Tone didn't respond. Juan sensed his terror and became aroused. There was something about blood that excited him.

"I guess he don't hear you, Uno," Kenyon teased. "What's up Tone? How you feeling, nigga?"

Tone still didn't respond, instead he closed his eyes.

"Naw nigga open yo muthafuckin eyes up. You knew you'd see us after what you did to Bro!"

Juan joked, "You giving this nigga too much credit, K. There's no way he thought he'd see us again. He already know what's up! This fuck nigga thought he could cross la familia and get away with it!"

Kenyon shook his head, "That was yo mans. We never even wanted to fuck with yo duck ass. Marc wanted to pull you out of the slums though."

"I didn't…" Tone tried to explain.

"Don't start lying bitch! What that nigga do to you huh? Answer that," Kenyon spazzed.

Tone started to shed tears, "My daughter man. I had to feed my daughter."

"Bullshit nigga! Everybody down with us eat. If shit was slow, you could've came to one of us."

Juan put a picture in front of Tone's face. "This daughter," he asked. The image showed a young girl with her throat slit. Ironically, she was dressed in an oversized t-shirt with Marcus's face on it.

When Tone saw the picture he immediately started to scream. Kenyon stood there in shock as well. He and Juan were in agreement about getting Tone, but he had no clue that Juan was going to kill Tone's daughter. Trying not to get distracted from the task at hand, Kenyon looked away from the picture and loaded his Tech 9 with an extended clip. Without any hesitation he riddled Tone's body with bullets.

The shots rang out and as each bullet hit, splatters of blood landed on the desk, floor and chair.

"My nigga," Juan gloated as Kenyon dropped the gun and walked away from the body.

Kenyon ignored Juan's cheering and walked into the bathroom to clean himself up. He was numb. All he could visualize were the pictures of Marcus that the detectives had. As a protector and provider, her felt responsible for Marcus's death. It was him who allowed Marcus to get into the game and he sent him to Memphis alone.

When Kenyon came out of the bathroom, Juan was playing with the dead body. "Aye Bro we should keep this nigga's eyes."

"Uno, you're sick! Real talk something really wrong with you my G."

Juan laughed, "Ain't nothing wrong with me. I just don't got no love in me for fuck niggas. I can't front, I don't do the emotions, but losing little bro fucked me up. It's only right we show out for him."

"I'm fucked up too, Dawg. Got me rethinking my whole shit. Like damn I can't believe I left him out there by his lonely to get smoked. Nigga. We getting too comfortable with this shit."

"You right Hermano, niggas definitely gotta tighten up."

Kenyon nodded, "Not just tighten up. It's time to start getting the fuck out."

Thirty-Eight

"Ro, let me call you back. I'm bout to wake Kenyon's ass up because these cats on some bull," Denise yelled.

Rochelle smacked her lips, " Girl I'm not bothering Juan's loco ass. That Mexican got him all jacked up."

Denise hung up the phone and filled a pot with some cold water. Once it was full, she carefully walked to the basement where Kenyon was sprawled out on the couch.

Swoosh! The water splashed as she soaked Kenyon.

"Are you crazy?" he yelled as he jumped up.

"I might be! Kenyon where have you been?"

Kenyon was furious, "Dee, leave me alone. You on some straight bullshit."

"I'm on some bull? You barely been home Kenyon in over a month. You're married with kids. What is this all about?'

"You don't think I know that?" he responded.

"I can't tell. You not out here moving like a married man."

Kenyon sensed how mad Dee was so he tried to defuse the situation, "I'm sorry."

"How long has it been going on?" she asked.

"What?"

Denise mumbled, "The affair."

Kenyon stood shirtless facing Denise, "Dee, I'm not cheating on you. I learned my lesson. All I'm doing is handling my business, trying to make sure shit sweet around here. I got a lot on me."

Denise could tell by the expression on Kenyon's face that something was bothering him, "What happened Kenyon? What did yall do?"

"Nothing."

"K, I know you," she explained.

"I know, Bae, but I need to leave the streets where they at. When I come home, I don't want to discuss that shit. My focus when I'm here is on us. I never want to lose you."

"So don't! Kenyon, I been yo rider since day one. This stuff is starting to be too much though. All of the late nights, being gone and sneaky stuff- I'm sick of it. You are a father and a husband. Juan can do that shit, you can't. I'm not trying to lose you either. Do you realize that Baby is dead and ain't never coming back? G left to raise Mari by herself. I never want that for KJ and Amire."

As strong as Kenyon appeared to be, on the inside he was broken. He tried to keep it together, but this time he couldn't. He laid his head on Denise's lap and broke down. Sobbing uncontrollably he could not contain himself. Denise held his head and rocked her legs comforting her man.

"Baby, its gone be okay," she assured him. Denise knew that Marcus's death was too much for Kenyon to handle. She also knew that the longer he stayed in the dope game, the more hurt they would endure. She wanted her husband out, even if that meant leaving Juan behind.

Thirty-Nine

"¡Hermana, Feliz Ano Nuevo!"

"Gracias. Te amo hermano," I replied.

"You sound just like Mamita, G. That shit is muy loco!"

I laughed, "Well she was my mother. It's sad because I wish we knew more about where we came from. It's 2007, I'll be twenty-two this year and don't know shit about my history."

"Estamos Mexicanos but we come from Sunnyside. Texas is our home and The Squad is our family," Juan explained.

"Of course I know that, but we have to still have family in Mexico. I've been looking through Mamita's photos and I don't know anybody in them."

"We can try to find them. Remember Manuel in Dallas? Papi said he was our primo. Maybe he knows where the rest of the family is. I can make some calls."

I was excited, "That would be cool."

"I'll have Rochelle look into it. Plus, we need another move anyway. Dallas would be a good look. It's time for us to get back to work."

"I'm not ready. For real, I'm cool on that other stuff, Juan."

Juan hesitated, " I know what happened to Marc was ill. Trust me it won't happen again, I promise. Vlad got a move in play that's gone set us for life."

"What about Mari?" I asked.

"Tio's baby gone always be straight. Everything I do is for her anyway."

I grabbed my phone to check the time. "I think Lex is bringing her home soon. She love going over there, but I'm making her come home for Amire's party."

"Damn, I forgot all about that. I gotta go get her something. Hopefully, Dee ain't on no trash."

"¿Que? ¿Por que dices eso?"

"Dee be acting funny like she don't want me around or something.

"Boy bye she knows you and K connected for life. She's probably just salty that you keep playing Ro."

"Man…they be on some bullshit, G. Rochelle trying to trap me and Dee probably putting the play down. I ain't no sucka."

I became defensive, " Juan stop with the games. You know that's your baby. Ro be down for you and now that she's pregnant you gotta be down for her too."

"I want a blood test- period. And while you lecturing me, what you plan on doing about Little Marcus. You know I wouldn't be a real nigga if I didn't start doing for him."

"You do what you need to do. I don't know how I really feel about the situation. To be honest I'm still hurt, but I know Marcus would want his kids together."

Juan hugged me, "I know that shit hurt, but you gone be okay. Just think about what it would be like if we didn't have each other. Marcus and Mari all that's left of him. They gotta be solid."

I responded, "I know."

"I'm gone bring him to the party tomorrow. The dirty hoe wont mind. I already warned her, but she said she just need help with him."

"For Marcus, I will at least try. If he was here we would probably have him anyway. This whole situation is still so crazy to me. You know Tone still ain't showed up in the hood?"

Juan shook his head, "That nigga ain't never coming back to Sunnyside."

I looked into Juan's eyes and I could see that he meant that. Everybody had been looking for Tone since Marcus died, but couldn't find him. I knew right then and there that my brother knew where he was. Loyalty was everything to Juan. A part of me was happy that Tone was dead, but that didn't change the fact that the love of my life was gone.

Forty

Amire's party was really nice. Dee and Kenyon made sure she had a great time. It was crazy hearing her call Dee "mommy". I always wondered how she would feel about the situation once she got older and found out the truth.

While we were partying, Juan had arrived with Marcus Jr. It bugged me out how much he looked like his father. Honestly, he looked more like him than Mari, who everyone thought was his twin. As much as I wanted to be mad, after looking at him, I couldn't be. I grabbed him out of Juan's arms and kissed him. When I looked at him, I saw Marcus, which made me want to love him. I was young and had a lot of growing up to do at the time, but I wanted to take the high road in that situation. Marcus Jr. belonged in our lives, even if that meant welcoming Bianca.

"He look just like that nigga, huh?" Kenyon stated while approaching us.

"Just like him, K."

Kenyon kissed me on the cheek, "I know it's not easy baby sis, but I'm proud of you. Hopefully, we can all work together to be there for him. He's family and I know Marcus would want that. Plus, I think it would be good for Mari's little grown ass to have her brother."

"She something else, man. I'm ready to give her away," I joked.

"She can't come here. I got enough estrogen in this joint. Naw, I'm playin'. Just know that you don't have to do this alone."

"¡Gracias!"

"Aye, don't start with that papi shit. Sounding like Juan."

I started cracking up, "Whatever! You know we Texicans and shit… Aye, can you take the kids to Juan for me? Tell him I will call him later on. I love yall."

I left the party going to meet Lillian and Britt. In school we used to hang out and kick it. They weren't a part of The Squad, but I considered them to be friends. Since Marcus' death they had been reaching out, so I decided to join them at a party.

That night I decided to hit the city in Marcus's Benz he had got before he died. Him, Juan and Kenyon had the same car to solidify their brotherhood. I loved riding it in, because it kept me close to them. The Forgiato rims were spinning as I glided through the parking lot. When I arrived, everybody seemed to be hanging outside.

Britt noticed me first and approached my car. "Damn, Griselda, you riding clean, Mami," she expressed.

As I opened the door I replied, "Thanks Britt. This was Marcus's whip."

"Aww…" she hugged me. "I know things been crazy. That's why we invited you out so you could have some fun and clear your mind."

"Already. You know I appreciate it, girl. Now where the drinks at?" I joked.

Britt escorted me into the party. I saw Lillian dancing with some guy on the dance floor. I waved and she acted as if she didn't want to wave back. *Fuck her* I thought to myself as we headed to the bar.

When we got there Britt introduced me, "Rome, this is my girl; Griselda."

The man grabbed my hand and kissed it, "Hello, Beautiful."

"Hi," I responded grabbing my hand quickly.

As we were exchanging a few words, Lillian walked up to us, "What's good, Rome? This party is whats up."

"Thanks. It finally feels good to be in Texas. It has been a long four months," he responded.

"Where are you from?" I asked trying to make conversation.

Lil cut in, "He from the A. Why?"

"Actually, I'm from Decatur. It's not too far from the city though."

I nodded. I wasn't trying to get too deep with him. Lillian's vibe let me know there was something going on between the two of them. I informed Britt that I was going to get some fresh air and headed to the patio.

Rome must've followed me. When I turned around he was standing there, "Don't pay her any attention. Lil is cool she's just stuntin on me."

"That's yo old lady?" I questioned.

He gave me this awkward look, "Ummm…not exactly! I ain't really trying to put her out there like that. Let's just say she helped welcome me to Texas."

"Got ya!"

"Single life gets lonely. I'm new to Texas so she just been providing me with some company."

I wasn't really interested in what he was saying, "You don't have to explain that to me. That's your business."

"Well I want to be in your business. Where your man at? If you belonged to me, you wouldn't be out this late."

I cut Rome off, "He's dead."

"I'm sorry to hear that," he replied.

I looked towards the car, "It's cool. He left me with a lot of good memories to hold close to my heart."

"Do ya'll have kids? If you don't mind me asking."

I hesitated, "Well we kind of got two. We have one together and he had another one while we were on a break."

"Oh okay that's cool."

Rome started cracking jokes on some drunk man cutting up on the patio. While we were laughing Britt approached the table. "Rome, its time to cut the cake. Everybody waiting on us inside."

"Happy Birthday, Rome," I said, grabbing my keys.

Britt looked surprised, "You leaving already, Griselda?"

"Yes, I'm tired. Thanks so much for inviting me love."

We hugged and I walked across the parking lot to my car. When I got in, I turned on Trill Fam's "Survival of the Fittest" and rolled out. Talking to Rome had me in my feelings. I was missing Marcus like crazy. Not only that but I was kind of interested in Rome. He was fine, easy to talk to and silly. I knew it was too early to be messing with a new dude, but there was a void in my life that needed to be filled.

Forty-One

"What took you so long?" Juan yelled.

"Don't start! I told you I had to do some shit today with Dee and the kids. What's wrong though? You been blowing my shit up all day," Kenyon responded.

"I caught that flight. When I got to the spot, there wasn't no car. I was shittin bricks, so I hurried up and copped a rental. Luckily, I had that ID on me. Boom…I hit Ox beater; no response. I called Marina but her line was disconnected. Nigga, I took a chance and hit Vlad's crib. Man, the Feds had the whole crib surrounded. K, on the kids, it looked like some shit from a movie."

Kenyon was shocked, "Damn! Only way they got to Vlad is through a snitch. It's gone be hell to pay out chea'."

"Hell yeah."

"So what now? We down to four birds mane. I sold the other two I had yesterday."

Juan smacked his forehead, "Nigga, I got a half left of boy and maybe a whole thang of drop. I'm bout to have Ro cut that shit so I can stretch it. We gotta find a new plug ASAP."

"You know I don't like new niggas. What about Vlad's people?"

After grabbing a folder out of the drawer, Juan replied, "Naw bro, we can't mess with nothing connected to Vlad. We don't know enough about his situation yet. We can't take those kind of chances."

"For real, that's another sign if you ask me. In the last six months, Marcus got smoked, Kane got knocked and now this shit with Vlad. Uno, that's too close to home."

Juan snapped, "Don't start that paranoid shit right now, K. I know Dee be on yo ass, but we gotta stick to the plan. Once we get this community center and stack some more bread we can get out. Our focus right now gotta be on finding a new plug though. And on some real shit, I can't do this without you."

"I got you nigga fa life, but time is ticking. I cant lose my old lady and kids, Uno. It aint worth it, fam."

"Speaking of kids, I need you to talk to Rochelle before I kill her ass. She getting on my damn nerves mane."

"Juan, you gotta chill on Ro. She pregnant and you know how they get when their emotions all fucked up. Ro a ride though and we need her," Kenyon pleaded.

"The problem is yo old lady! She want what y'all got and it's fucking up our whole thang!"

Kenyon grabbed his phone, "Nigga, we been selling drugs since we been kids. We got whips, businesses, nice cribs and shit. None of this would mean nothing without Dee and my kids. You almost twenty-seven. It's time for you to have something other than the dope game."

"Who you? Dr. Phil? I'm on this bread, but you right. I'm gone do something special for the bitch since she got my seed."

"That's what I'm saying. If she ain't right, yo seed ain't right."

Juan slapped hands with Kenyon, "Aye, this her calling right now. I got a few moves to make. I'll check you out later."

"Already," Kenyon stated leaving Juan's place.

"Sup Mamita?" Juan asked closing the door behind Kenyon.

Rochelle asked, "Are you busy? Your child got me over here starving."

"Naw, I was just fucking with K. for a minute. What you want to eat?"

"I want some kind of pasta. Italian or some shit," she responded.

"I'll be over in a second. Make sure you wear something I like too. I might wanna slide my hand up yo dress feel me?"

Rochelle was feeling Juan's vibe, " I'm with it. So, I'm guessing you're ready to make this thing official?"

"You got my child in you. Y'all both belong to me. I ain't into all the emotional shit, but I'm gone do right by yall."

"I hear you," Rochelle stated trying to compose herself.

"I'll be through in a second, so get dressed," Juan demanded.

Despite how he acted, Juan was extremely excited to have a child. He prayed for a son, so he could give him the game like Papi had done for him. Rochelle's pregnancy reminded him of what his childhood was like. It was filled with love and laughter, something his soul needed to balance out the grit from the streets.

Part Five

Forty-Two

October 9, 2007, Rochelle gave birth to Juan Ca'Marcus Gonzales. They decided to name him after Marcus and Papi. The name was ghetto, but it meant so much to us all.

When I got the call, I was in the middle of doing some last minute cleaning at the community center. Juan and Kenyon purchased the building from the foreclosure list. To make the money seem legit, they got a bank loan. Denise even applied for some state grants. The funds helped hire contractors who revamped the place. Collectively, we decorated and designed the rooms. In my opinion, the center was one of the nicest places in Sunnyside. I was proud to be apart of the process. Not to mention we had decided to dedicate the center in Marcus's honor. When we were younger, he loved playing basketball and hanging at The Drop. This was our way of paying homage to his legacy.

"What took you so long?" Juan asked when I finally arrived at the hospital.

"Negro, do you not see me? I've been cleaning at the center all day. I haven't even laid eyes on my own child."

Juan gloated, "That joint lit, G. The kids gone love that shit."

"I already know, especially my sobrino. Where is he?"

"They took my little homie to get his jawn whacked. Rochelle in a lot of pain from that c-section. The doctors doped her up; now she sleep."

As Juan and I waited for the doctors to bring the baby back, I got a text from Rome. *I miss you* it read.

Since meeting at his party, we had been texting a lot. Although I really didn't know Rome, I enjoyed his conversation. We talked about everything. Ironically, he gave me a lot of advice to help with my grief over Marcus's death.

Juan noticed the grin on my face while exchanging words with Rome and he started poking fun at me, "Who got yo head all in the clouds?"

"Shut up! It's just my friend Rome."

"Old dude from Georgia?" he questioned.

I was confused because I had never mentioned meeting Rome to Juan.

"Don't be looking all stupid now. I know about everything you do. For real, I don't know much about old dude so be careful. He's Britt people, but you know she known to be shady."

"Juan, we are just friends. He's just somebody I talk to; nothing more, nothing less."

"I dig. Just make sure you don't get sidetracked. Remember what the fuck we doing," he demanded.

Kenyon and Dee walked up as we were fussing. "La Familia," Kenyon yelled.

"Comrade," Juan responded dapping Kenyon up.

"Hey ya'll," I stated hugging Dee.

"Dee, they got Ro on some meds and she knocked out. Mommy left like an hour ago. We're just waiting on Lil' Uno to come back from the circumcision," Juan explained.

Dee was excited about the baby. "Okay cool! We just gone wait here with y'all. Ken, can you go to the vending machines and grab me a Sprite?

"I got you, Bae. Uno, come fuck with me," Kenyon demanded.

Once they were away from us he started talking, "Word around the way is some undercovers been in the hood asking questions. Mook said a nigga came in the shop to get a cut asking who the plug was. I pulled the cameras to see what the nigga looked like. Pee ran the license plates, but the shit came back bogus."

"Damn! Now's a bad time for the fuckin feds to show they face. Me and G hitting Dallas next week to check out my primo. Manuel got the same plug that Papi started out with. I'm talking about warehouses full of everything we need!"

"Dig dat! We definitely need a power move, but you think now's a good time? I think we should lay low and find out what's going on in the hood first."

Juan grabbed his phone, "Remember the white bitch that's always trying to throw me the pussy?"

"Yeah, she the police though."

"She work in forensics investigating murders and shit."

Kenyon questioned, "Okay? What about her?"

"She got access to everything we need. I'm gone hit her up and see how she moving. I need you to steal her computer. I bet Pee can hack it and we can see what's up."

Kenyon nodded, " That's cool. We gotta stay one step ahead of these clowns. Our shit solid. The only way they get to us is through a snitch- flatout."

"Already! We gone find out who singing. I'm gone end that shit off dribble. This a real man's game, ain't no room for rats."

"Give them niggas cheese and rock em to sleep ya dig? Right now though, we gotta focus on the baby and getting this center open. That should shift everybody's attention off us."

"Fa sho! Aye, I want you to talk to Dee about selling the diners. I got some other investments I want to make that's gone bring us more bread and less attention."

"I don't know, Bro. Business is booming in Atlanta. We already doubled our bread. It wouldn't be wise to sell now. Matter of fact, Dee told me that King Enterprises offered to buy it from us. We can work out some kind of partnership with them and let them be upfront. Shit, we just fall back and collect the paper."

Juan laughed, "Dee got you polished up nigga. Talking about partnerships and shit. She don't be playing about her bread. That's fa sho."

"She really be on it. Her slick ass probably stashing her cash in case she leave a nigga. I'm gone be living off noodles and shit while she in the hills eating lobster."

Although they found humor is Denise's hustle, Kenyon feared what that meant for their marriage. He knew that Denise was serious about leaving Texas and starting over. If he didn't start making the right moves, his life could be on the line.

Forty-Three

When I arrived at The Marcus Murray Community Center, I was overwhelmed with emotion. Despite being heartbroken that Marcus was gone, I was very happy about the center. October 20th was a good day for us all.

The news reporters, the mayor and the people of Sunnyside showed out. When I looked around, there was nothing but love. Juan had managed to hire a few artists to perform at the opening and I knew Sunnyside would appreciate that. Our hood was built like a family for real.

Neither Juan nor Kenyon wanted to be photographed or on the news. So of course Dee and I were photographed with our liaison Kim Jones. She assisted with the day-to-day operations of the center. Dee handled all of the paperwork and business. I was responsible for the kids and making sure everything was running smoothly. Staffing was also my responsibility. I hired Alexis and a few other ladies I knew from the hood to help out. One of Dee's uncles was our maintenance man and bus driver. We started off small, but everything was in place.

After the newspaper arrived, we gathered in front of the door to cut the ribbon. I looked out into the crowd and noticed Bianca and MJ standing next to Rochelle. I had Dee stall the process for a minute while I went to speak to Bianca. "Hey Bianca."

She looked uncomfortable, " What's up, Griselda?"

"We bout to cut the ribbon with Marcus's name on it. I want MJ to be up there with us, if you don't mind."

"My son not about to be there without me," she snapped.

I knew that it wasn't the time or place for drama so I agreed. "That's fine! Just bring your simple ass on. Today is about Marcus and his legacy, not you or me."

Bianca followed behind me as I headed towards the entrance. Honestly, I didn't mind her being up there. She was busted! Since Marcus's death she had fallen off. Uno told me that she was on powder real bad. I didn't feel bad though, I felt like maybe it was karma.

The Mayor spoke, "At this time we as a community would like to welcome the Marcus Murray Community Center to Sunnyside, Texas." Everybody in the crowd went nuts as she continued, "With me is the family and children of the late Marcus Murray."

She handed me the microphone, "Sunnyside, we appreciate all of the love. This center is for us and ours. Please enjoy. And to the love of my life, Marcus Murray, rest easy." When I was done talking, I handed the microphone to Alexis who had just arrived.

"Thank you all for keeping my son's memory alive. This community helped raise him and I am forever grateful. To my beautiful grandchildren, I love you all. Marcus, my child, rest peacefully. God bless you all."

Alexis was the last person to speak. The crowd interrupted her, when Pimp C hopped out of a black Suburban in front of the center. Houston loved Pimp; he was a Texas legend. Juan had told me that he used to serve Pimp, but I didn't believe him. I was in awe that he came out to support the center.

The crowd rushed Pimp as soon as he got out of the car. His security was pushing people back so that he could make it to the performance area. Once he arrived, Juan motioned for Dee to hand him the microphone. "It's ya folk Sweet Jones Jr! I got my brother Bun with me ya dig. We out chea to show some H-Town love to our patna Marcus. Let's take it back."

After the beat dropped they started rapping, "Back front and side to side. I got a 64 Chevy in my yard. A drop top pearl paint job is hard. White plush inside southern robe is fresh. Triple gold-double a daytons is the best…" As UGK rhymed people were singing every word. I even caught Juan's mean ass smiling and jamming along.

UGK had everybody on ten. When their performance was over, there was a pause in the music for a few minutes. I assumed something was wrong then I heard, "He greets his father with his hands out. Rehabilitated slightly, glad to be the man's child. The world is different since he seen it last. Out of jail, been seven years, but he's happy that he's free at last."

I turned and looked at Kenyon, "Not Face though?" I damn near fainted. Scarface was Marcus's favorite rapper. We used to listen to the Geto Boys for hours. I remember one time we ran into Bill at the Galleria and Marcus was acting like a groupie. I teased him every time I thought about that day. Man, we had some good times. I missed Marcus so much and looking at how Ken and Juan were rocking, I knew I wasn't alone.

"Now this what I'm talking about," stated Dee as she danced with Baby Uno in her arms.

"This is definitely the shit, Sis. He would've been on ten knowing that Face and UGK were rocking in the hood. Damn!"

Kenyon wrapped his arms around me, "G, you see this shit? Look at all the love we getting out chea' for Marcus. Sunnyside know we always been solid and this hood is home. It's love here like no other place. I'm proud of this shit."

Dee agreed, "This is one of them moments where we get to see the fruits of our labor. We worked extremely hard to get this center up and running. So many kids' lives will be forever changed from that. To me, that makes this shit worth it."

Most people would probably criticize the fact that The Squad brought hood rappers to perform at the opening for a community center. However, the H-Town story was so much deeper than that. Children and adults in the ghetto shared the same struggle and pain. Fortunately, music was one of the few things that gave us all hope. Knowing that Pimp, Face and Bun were from our same walk and made it out was life changing.

Of course we were using the dope game as our means of getting out, but we didn't know any other way. Truth be told, our hustle benefited the same community we served. We gave the kids in our community a safe haven. The center was filled with books, computers, toys, and everything else they needed. Juan even bought clean clothes and shoes to have for those kids in need. Kenyon had the barbers set up to provide free haircuts once a week. Denise and I hired tutors and we also put up money to help families with financial hardships. Bottomline, we loved our hood and the people in it. Sunnyside made us and we were trying to give all that love back.

Forty-Four

Juan had got in touch with Manuel, who invited us down to visit. When Juan said I couldn't bring Mari, I knew we were going to handle business. I wanted to see our primo and learn more about the family so I wasn't tripping. Before we left I agreed to meet Rome for breakfast.

"Buenos Dias," he greeted me pulling out my chair when I reached the table.

I giggled, "Buenos Dias Señor."

Rome bragged, "I've been practicing my Spanish."

"I see you!"

Rome ordered us two mimosas. "Thank you for meeting me."

"No problem. What's up with you though?" I asked.

"Nothing much for real. I'm planning a trip back home for my mom's 55th birthday party. I was thinking that you could come with me?"

Surprised, I didn't know what to say so I just looked at him.

"What's wrong?" he questioned.

"Rome, you're cool and all, but I'm not single."

He looked confused. "Hold up! You're in a relationship?"

"Marcus and I have this bond. I never want to be disloyal to him."

"Griselda, he's dead. I don't really understand what you're talking about."

I felt like a bullet pierced my heart. I knew that Marcus wasn't physically alive, but I also never really grasped that he was gone and never coming back. Rome's words caught me off guard and I could not hold back my tears. Never once did I ever consider moving on with my life. All I knew was the love Marcus and I shared and it meant everything to me. That's all I had left of him and I never wanted to let that go. "I'm sorry," I mumbled to Rome.

"You don't have to say sorry. To a degree I understand where you're coming from," he expressed.

"You do?"

He explained, "I understand the trauma from losing somebody you love. It takes time to heal. I just want you to know that loving your child's father doesn't mean you have to die with him. You are a human and you deserve to be happy again. I'm sure he would want that for you."

I nodded my head, but didn't respond.

"I do need to ask though, what do you call what we're doing?"

"I like you Rome, but I'd be lying if I said it didn't make me uncomfortable."

Rome pulled his chair close to mine, " What if I said that I was falling in love with you? Griselda, I want you to be my woman. I can help you heal the hurt. Take a chance with me?"

"I'm scared," I muttered.

"I promise I won't hurt you. All I need is a chance to prove that to you."

Being honest I really did like Rome and wanted to have a man in my life. However, I was terrified. With the shit Juan was into, I never knew people's motives. One time a guy was plotting on robbing Juan so he tried to date me to get close to him. Juan ended up breaking his ribs. I didn't want anything to happen like that again. Rome seemed different so I decided that I wanted him to meet Juan and Kenyon.

"How about this? When I come from visiting my family, I'll let you meet my brothers. They gotta give this the okay."

Rome smiled, "I'm with it!"

"Alright...I gotta go though. I will text you later."

Rome escorted me to my car after paying the bill. Twenty minutes later, I arrived at Rochelle's house. Juan, Kenyon, and the baby were outside on the porch chilling.

"Nice of you to join us," Juan teased.

"Shut up! I'm on time fool. Y'all ready to go?"

Rochelle walked on the porch, "This about to be a long ass ride in this heat."

"You're coming with us, Ro," I asked.

Juan cut her off, "Yeah they coming with us."

"So why couldn't I bring Mari?"

"Come on now, G," Juan smirked.

I was annoyed. One of the rules we always followed was that the kids were never to be around the drugs. Juan hadn't ran his plan by me, but I assumed we were going to get a pack. That meant that it was a kid free ride. Not only was I pissed that we were taking the baby, but I was mad that I didn't know what we were heading into. In typical Juan fashion, it was his way or no way.

"G, we got Mari don't trip," Kenyon assured me.

"I know she's in good hands, Bro. Thank you."

Grabbing my bag, I sat in the back seat waiting on them to get their things into the car. As we headed up Interstate 45, I played with my nephew and tried to forget how mad I was. Rochelle drove and Juan sat in the passenger seat looking at properties. Almost four hours later we arrived at Manuel's house. I vaguely remembered the scenery from my childhood. It was a typical Dallas ranch. There were bullheads and flags plastered throughout the yard. When we pulled into the gravel, Manuel was sitting on the porch sipping a Modelo Beer. He stood about five feet tall, with an orange tan and buzz cut. What made him stand out most was the gold fronts he had in his mouth.

Manuel approached the car holding his arms up, "Bienvenido La Familia."

"Primo," Juan yelled.

"Hola Manuel," I chimed in.

Rochelle waved because she didn't know any Spanish.

"Ven," Manuel instructed and we followed behind him.

We headed inside of the home. I thought I was hallucinating. On the outside the home looked raggedy, but on the inside it was laid out. The floors were marble as well as the kitchen countertops. The windows were stained-glass like those in the church. I noticed a few gold statues of the Virgin Mary. Manuel directed us to the family room. There were a few flat screens hanging from the wall, a fully stocked bar, pool table and huge sectionals. His wife had prepared food and drinks for us.

"How y'all doing family?"

"Primos, this is my wife, Sandy. She got some things together for y'all. Please help yourselves."

I was surprised to see Manuel's wife. She was about 5'1 with a slim-thick build. Her hair was in a huge, curly afro. I was most captivated by her skin tone. We grew up around black people, but she was a lot darker. Her complexion reminded me of dark chocolate. It was beautiful.

"Griselda," I stuck my hand out.

"Girl we give hugs around here," she said grabbing me as we giggled.

Juan looked so delighted, "This is what family is all about. Y'all enjoy!"

"I see margaritas. We're definitely going to enjoy ourselves," Rochelle joked.

We unfolded the baby's playpen and laid him down for a nap. Sandy turned on Geto Boys and we started kicking it. I felt right at home.

Forty-Five

"Morning, Bro."

"What's going on around here?" Kenyon asked.

"Nothing much just keeping shit steady feel me?" Mook replied.

Kenyon grabbed a bottled water and sat down, "So what's up with the 911?"

"Old dude I told you about is definitely the Feds. Tito was in here running his mouth yesterday. The homie said that old dude was talking to twelve in the back of Dave's spot. You know them niggas got popped."

"I heard his bitch narked on him over some cheating shit."

Mook started laughing, " Man…she not only sent them to the spot, but she gave them all the work he had at her crib. Dave put a number on her skull. Ain't nobody seen her in a cool little minute."

"You cant trust these hoes, that's why I'm never leaving my old lady. These chicks out here moving foul. Especially these chicken heads using their pussy for a come up."

"Hell yeah! I been with Meesha for ten years. Soon as she polish up, I'm gone change her name for sure."

"You gotta train her, Mook. I seen Meesh on video putting the paws on somebody a few weeks ago. Shit, put some bread in her face to shift her focus."

"K, you might be on to something. Speaking of bread though, I got a bug for you. Word is Dave was bringing niggas names up. On some shit like I'm small time, the real plug is that nigga Uno."

Kenyon was pissed. "Oh word? Thanks for letting me know. We definitely gone look into that shit. Old pussy ass niggas."

"I already know. Do me a favor though. Don't let anybody other than Uno know where you got that from. This shop is my gateway to the streets. I like niggas feeling comfortable with spilling their guts in here."

Kenyon gave Mook dap, "Already."

When he left the shop, Kenyon texted Juan their code for an emergency. Soon as he reached the stop sign, he noticed a black Ford Taurus following him. He immediately snapped the burner in half. Luckily, he had left his main phone at home on the dresser. As expected, the officer turned on his sirens and pulled Kenyon over.

As the officer approached the car, Kenyon rolled down the window, " Hello, Officer."

"License and registration," he demanded.

While grabbing his credentials, Kenyon asked, " May I ask why I'm being stopped?"

The officer ignored Kenyon's request. Instead he took his paperwork back to the cruiser to verify. Kenyon sat in the car waiting for at least ten minutes. When the officer finally returned, he handed Kenyon his license.

"Watch your back. We're coming for Uno," the officer stated.

Kenyon gave the officer a cold look before peeping his badge. His name was Officer Winston. Based on what had just taken place, Kenyon knew that they were being targeted by the police and he was ready to strap up.

Kenyon made sure he stopped a few times before heading towards his neighborhood. The detectives were known to follow people and case their homes. He decided to park his car in the neighborhood and walk home. When he arrived he called Denise into the basement, " Bae, come holla at me for a second."

"Why you looking like that?" Dee asked when she entered the basement.

"Mook hit me up like 'swing by the shop.' Last week he said some police ass nigga was around the shop asking questions. They spot this same dude behind Dave's spot talking to a detective. Mind you, Dave just got popped. Word is he told them that he was the wrong guy. Uno was the plug."

"Dave been hating and you know that. I don't care how much y'all love Sunnyside, everybody don't love y'all back. Period!"

"It gets worse. Soon as I'm leaving the shop, I get blooped. I wasn't even speeding or nothing. The pig run my shit- of course it's clean. He come back to the car and say 'watch your back, we're coming for Uno.'"

Denise sat down in a chair, "Ken, this is getting crazy. All bullshit aside, it's definitely time to get things in order so we can blow this shit."

"Bae you're right. I got a bad feeling about all of this shit. We gotta start making different moves. How much money in the wall?"

"Last time I counted it was like 1.8. Everybody's boxes had 250 bands in them. The shop's account has ten thousand and the restaurant had like 200, but we hadn't done payroll yet."

Kenyon grabbed his briefcase and handed Dee a set of keys. " I want you to move the 1.8 to our stash spot. Just in case they start watching this bitch. What's in our personal account?"

"Hold up," Denise grabbed her iPad. "There is almost twelve thousand in my savings and about six in my checking."

"Bet. Don't touch nothing else. Just move the 1.8 because we can account for everything else. Your checks can cover all of our bills so we straight."

Denise nodded, "That's why I always stress to you the importance of saving our bread. In order for us to stay under the radar, we gotta live modestly. We got these kids to think about. On the up and up, I want to take Griselda with us as well. They don't have any family just us. Marcus would want them to be close to us."

"I already know. I've been thinking and I'm excited about Atlanta. LA is cool to vacation, but I think the south is a better fit for us. We can get like a timeshare or something there for when we want to vacation. What you think?"

"I'm with it, K, as long as we not stuck in Texas. Hell, I could even get my Masters Degree in Georgia. The restaurant is there as well so it works."

Kenyon took off his shirt, " I ain't gone lie, I want to get a business degree so I can really do my thang. With us both having them under our belts, we should be able to really boss up."

Denise leaned over and kissed Kenyon in the mouth before heading towards the steps. As she walked away, he couldn't help but stare at her ass. She was throwing her hips purposely to entice him. Before she left the basement, Kenyon stopped her.

"Get naked," he demanded.

Right there on the steps Denise undressed while her eyes were locked on Kenyon standing there with a hard dick ready for action.

Forty-Six

We had an amazing time in Dallas with Manuel and Sandy. They cooked; we drank and looked at old pictures. Manuel had pictures of Abuela and her hermanos. I enjoyed seeing my family. Despite being separated for so long, we agreed to keep in touch moving forward. Manuel even said he was going to host a family reunion so that we could see everybody.

"Hi, Auntie's man," I cooed holding the baby in the backseat. He was identical to my brother as a baby. Rochelle was light skinned, but the baby had a Mexican tan.

"Uno, can you drive?" Rochelle requested. "Sandy got me lit with those damn ritas."

Juan smirked, " Man, damn! Aye G, why don't you whip real quick?"

"Hell naw. I'm riding with my baby."

Rochelle laughed, "You having Mari fever huh?"

"Girl, you already know. I can't wait to get my girl. Have you talked to Dee?"

"I talked to them earlier. The girls were playing dress up and Dee was fussing about the toys being all over her living room."

As we pulled off, Juan demanded I text Kenyon. "Tell him to meet us at the spot. I know that nigga in the gym so he should be done when we get there."

I joked, "You need to be there too, fat ass."

"Don't come for mines. My baby daddy cold, " Rochelle responded.

"Whatever," I yelled laying my head on the armrest. As we rode I watched the baby struggle to eat his feet. The entire ride he blew bubbles, babbled and hit me with his toys. I loved my nephew, but I was happy when we finally arrived back home.

When we pulled in, I ran as fast as I could into the house to find Mari.

"She knocked out, G," Dee advised.

"I don't care. I'm bout to wake her up. She in Amire room?"

Dee smacked her lips, "You coming in here ruining nap time. Mari threw up earlier. She's actually laying across my bed. Her and Amire been on my heels."

"I'll be glad when they get gone. I can't even get a feel in," Kenyon joked as he walked in on our conversation.

"Nigga, where you been? You knew we were coming!"

Kenyon grabbed a water out of the fridge, "I was at the gym. I know y'all just got here. Let's rock though."

Juan followed Kenyon into their office space.

"What's the word? Why you looking like that, Patna?"

Kenyon made sure the door was closed, "Man…not only is some nigga asking around in the hood, but that same dude got spotted outside of Dave spot with the detectives. Little bro tell me when Dave got smacked he tell them like what y'all want me for, Uno the nigga with the weight. Today, I'm leaving the shop and I get pulled over soon as I pull out. The pig run my shit and come back and say 'watch yo back. We coming for UNO.'"

Surprisingly, Juan started laughing which threw Kenyon off.

"No worries, Comrade. Dave a hoe nigga. He just started a war and don't even know it."

"Bro, we can't kill Dave right now. If something happens to him, they gone really be on our heels. We gotta let this shit die down before we bust a move."

"Ain't no mercy on a nigga bringing my name up to them people. Fuck you thought?" Juan questioned.

"Now is not the time for the bullshit. We need a plan, a solid fucking plan. Don't start this impulse shit."

Juan stood up, " We gone off these niggas and take our shit elsewhere. Period!"

"Nigga everywhere we go it's some shit. In Maryland, G got hemmed up. Marcus got killed in Memphis. We was cool in the A, but Vlad got fucked. Now this shit here. Use your head."

"You being a real pussy right now, Kenyon. Pull yo skirt up nigga! You know thats all a part of the game."

Kenyon stood up and faced Juan, " Fuck what you talkin bout. I got kids. The only goal we had was to get this money and get the fuck out the way."

"No witnesses and no evidence! No fuckin jail time. You already know how we rocking."

"Fuck all that. Look, I'm getting out of this shit sooner than later. The game then gave me all it has to offer. We then became millionaires in this shit. It's time to bounce. Sooner or later we bound to hit the choppin block."

Juan snapped, "So you just gone leave me out here solo?"

Kenyon approached Juan, "I ain't never not had you fuck you talkin bout? The problem is you too reckless. That's the same shit that got Marcus killed. I told you he wasn't ready for Memphis. Nah, you always gotta call the shots. I'll be damned if you get me hemmed up nigga. "

"That's how you feel Puta? You on this familia shit tough. I'm the reason you have the means to take care of them. Don't get it twisted. If anything you should be paying homage to me like you pray to God," Juan screamed.

"Bitch, fuck you! You ain't God!" Kenyon started to yell. He couldn't control himself and punched Juan in the face.

Wiping the blood from his lip Juan smiled, "That's all you got huh? Hitting me ain't gone change the fact that I made you."

As the commotion erupted, Denise rushed to the office to see what was going on. When she opened the door, Kenyon and Juan were toe to toe.

"What the hell is going on in here?" she asked.

Juan looked at Dee and stated, "You took my brother away from me. That's what the fuck is going on."

Denise looked at Kenyon, "What is going on?"

"Fuck that nigga!"

Things got out of hand with Juan and Kenyon. They always had disagreements, but they were always small. This situation escalated and none of us knew what was going to happen. At that moment I knew that The Squad's love and loyalty was being tested.

Forty-Seven

With everything going on in Houston, I decided to go to Georgia with Rome. For the first time since my parents split, I felt like I was losing my family. Rome became my comfort.

"Hello," I answered.

"Baby, what's taking you so long?" it was Rome on the phone.

"I'm pulling up now. I had to take the kids to their grandmother's house. Look out the window."

"Oh so you just gone stunt on me in the Range huh? How my old lady riding cleaner than I am," Rome joked.

I laughed, "You see I had to get my baby washed."

Rome came down the stairs of his apartment shirtless. He was very good looking. He stood over six feet tall; solid. His skin was dark like a Hershey bar and his teeth were white as snow. I thought his beard was what really made him sexy. His eyes were hazel and they were enticing. It had been a while since I had sex and everything about him turned me on. Georgia is where I planned on solidifying things.

"Hey beautiful," he kissed me on the cheek. "You ready for this trip?"

"Heck yeah, I need to get away. My brother said you better take good care of me."

Rome nodded, " What happened to him coming to meet me? I've been waiting."

"Oh trust me you'll meet his crazy butt. He's been busy working though."

While he was grabbing my bags, Rome laughed sarcastically.

"What's funny?"

"Griselda, I wouldn't say what he does is work."

I snapped, "By that, you mean what?"

"I was joking; please relax."

"I don't know what you got going on, but don't ever come for my brother. That's my life and whoever you getting your information from need to get it right!"

"Look, my cousin mentioned to me that your brother wasn't nothing to mess with. She said he was a real gangster around here. I apologize for assuming. Its not my business how he lives his life. All I know is I expressed to someone that I really liked you and they told me to be careful. There was nothing more or less to the conversation," he explained.

"Rome you better be careful with that, especially in Texas. People die over rumors. Only speak on what you know and maybe not even that. Just make sure you're not mentioning my brother. I like you and we don't need them kind of problems."

As annoyed as I was with Rome, Brit had every right to warn him about Juan. My brother was dangerous and he did not play about his loved ones. I definitely didn't want any issues with them, so I had to warn Rome. If Juan got wind of him talking like that, it would've been bad.

Rome must've sensed that I was uneasy, "Griselda, I'm sorry for real. I know how much your brother means to you. I don't want that to ruin anything we got going on. It's gone be a good time in Georgia and you get to meet my mom."

"Its cool. You should go get dressed. Otherwise, we are going to miss our flight."

While Rome got ready, I called Alexis and checked on the kids. I also scheduled some field trips for the center. Despite all of the craziness around me, I took pride in the center and the kids. Being with the kids made me happier than anything.

"You ready?" Rome interrupted my daze.

"Leggo," I replied.

When we arrived, the plane was boarding. I was nervous as hell, so I ordered some wine to help me relax. I had never really been introduced to anyone's mother before. Alexis didn't count because we were family.

"You good Babe?" Rome asked

"Yes, I'm fine. Kind of nervous but I think everything will be okay. They are going to love me or they are going to hate me," I shrugged.

Rome grabbed my hand, "They are going to love you. You gone have to make some Spanish rice to seal the deal though. That's the winner right there."

"I'm on vacation. The only thing you should be focused on eating is me."

"We can make that happen too. Shoot, we mess around and get married while we down there."

Sticking my ring finger out I yelled, "A cool three karats would be nice."

"Girl, you gone have me working all kind of overtime to pay for that. A nigga gone be eating oodles and noodles for months," Rome joked.

Forty-Eight

It had been a week since Kenyon and Juan's fallout. Juan felt betrayed and Kenyon felt that Juan was inconsiderate of his feelings. Both men were operating with prideful egos, therefore they kept their distance. However, Kenyon was still determined to take care of business.

Surprisingly, he was able to break into Officer Winston's car. He had been following him, to learn his movements. Kenyon noticed that he frequently met up with the undercover agent that had been to the shop. He also realized that the barbershop, community center and one of their trap houses were being watched. Typically, Kenyon and Juan would handle these situations together, but this time Kenyon was on his own.

One particular night, Kenyon decided to follow Winston home from a bar. Apparently, he had a nasty coke habit. After his shift, he headed to the hood to cop drugs. As Winston staggered into his apartment, he accidentally left his car unlocked. Kenyon covered his face and gloved his hands before he entered the vehicle and took all of the folders and a computer.

"Bro, meet me at the chop shop. It's an emergency," Kenyon stated before hanging up the phone.

Julio arrived at the warehouse annoyed that Kenyon woke him up, " This better be good, K. Dot. My bitch trippin."

"I promise she'll be good when you go home with this bag. I need you to break this laptop and remove the tracker. This phone gotta be disabled too."

Julio grabbed the devices, "Where you get this shit from? Oh hell naw, nigga. This twelve shit."

"How you know?" Kenyon questioned.

"Government devices have special serial numbers. They have extra firmware on them too, to stop hackers. The problem is there are a lot of dirty cops, so niggas got hipped to the game."

"So can you get this done?"

"Oh yeah this gone be easy, Fam. Whoever you got this joint from has the enhanced security disabled. I got a file transporter so we can wipe this bitch and destroy it. I'll put the files on a clean drive. Just make sure you never get caught with it."

Kenyon nodded in agreement, "Bet."

Within a few hours, Julio was completely done with the job. He gave Kenyon a flash drive that contained the files and burned both devices. Before leaving the warehouse, Kenyon gave Julio three thousand dollars contained in rubber bands.

"I sit alone in my four-cornered room, starin at candles, oh that shit is on, let me drop some shit like this here, real smooth. At night I cant sleep, I toss and turn. Candlesticks in the dark, visions of bodies bein' burned…" the Geto Boys blasted through the speakers. Kenyon was emotionally drained.

When he arrived at home, he decided to have a drink. He went into the basement only to find Dee sitting at the bar drinking wine.

"What are you doing up?" he asked.

"I guess I could ask you the same thing," she smirked.

Kenyon grabbed a chair, "Why you looking like that, Dee?"

"You promised me that we were leaving this life behind, Kenyon. It's not looking like we're going anywhere anytime soon."

"I told you we're getting out of here. I promise Dee. That's what I'm working on now. We getting this bread all the way right and I gotta make sure Juan good. After that baby we on our way."

Denise started banging on the bar, " Fuck Juan! That muthafucka don't mean nobody good, Kenyon. Did you know that the baby is upstairs? Huh? I bet you also didn't know that Rochelle got arrested in the middle of the night."

"Hold up what?"

"This chick got caught on the road leaving Dallas with three keys of white boy. According to Mommy, she was speeding so they pulled her over. I don't know what the fuck Rochelle was thinking, Kenyon. She had a fuckin gun on her. This ain't Ro! She doing all of this silly shit to please Juan."

Kenyon's heart sank in. He couldn't even articulate his thoughts. Instead he just walked over to his wife and embraced her. All of the years they had been doing dirt; he never imagined that one of their loved ones would get caught up. Not only did he feel bad, but he also felt responsible. Rochelle met Juan through him. She stepped up because he stepped down.

Forty-Nine

Denise and I sat in the courtroom waiting for Rochelle to be arraigned. I had never been inside of a courthouse before. The people were rude and made us feel as if we did something wrong. When they called Rochelle's name a burly cop escorted her out. Her feet were shackled in chains and her hands were cuffed in front of her stomach. Rochelle's hair was always laid, but this day she looked like a fiend. What stood out to me the most was her face. It was swollen and bright red. We could tell that she had been doing a lot of crying. My heart broke for Rochelle, realizing that it could've been me.

"Your honor, the defendant is charged with a criminal felony for possession of a controlled substance, a weapon under disability, speeding, drug trafficking and resisting arrest," the prosecutor stated.

"How do you plead, Ms. Jones?" the judge asked.

Rochelle plead not guilty and was given a court date for pretrial. The prosecutor was vicious. She asked the judge to deny Rochelle a bond, but since it was her first offense the judge denied the request. He released her on home restriction with a two hundred and fifty thousand dollar bond.

Dee was relieved that her bond was at least doable for the family. Their mother's home was worth almost two hundred thousand dollars and she agreed to put it up for collateral. Juan was ducked off at a hotel waiting to pay Ro's bond as well.

As soon as we left court, we headed to the hotel. I knew Dee wasn't feeling Juan so I tried to make things a little better.

"Dee, you know that Juan is gonna do everything he needs too in order to get Ro off," I explained.

"Look G, I know you're worried about us. I promise I wont kill Juan. I'm just really mad at him right now. Yo other brother on my shit list too. I'm tired of this street shit. It's time for them to figure out what's next."

"I'm with you. It's definitely time for a change. We've been saying that!"

Juan opened the door for us when we arrived at the room.

"What happened?" Kenyon asked as soon as we entered the room.

Denise pushed past Juan, "Hello to you too husband," she stated sarcastically.

Just as Kenyon and Dee started bickering, her phone rang. She walked into the bathroom to finish her call.

"Y'all should've seen Ro. She almost had us in tears. We gotta get her out of this man. Ro ain't built for the joint. Ken, Mommy told Dee she would put up the house."

"That might be the move. It keeps the heat off of us and gets Ro out. I got the bread I can stash away just in case. I already paid the lawyer the ten bands, so we good right now," Juan celebrated.

"Who good?" Dee asked coming out of the bathroom.

"We all good. What you mean?" he replied.

"I'm just not understanding how you're so happy and my sister shackled in chains! Please help me understand how you're good and your son's mother caught a FED case, Juan."

I interrupted, "Please don't start y'all. Now is not the time."

"I agree," Kenyon stated.

"Naw, man. Fuck what y'all talking bout! Dee act like she got an issue with me and y'all know it. You don't think Rochelle tell me the shit you say, Fam? Damn, you more worried about me than my own bitch. Fuck is the deal?" Juan taunted.

"Aye nigga chill! That's my wife. We ain't even about to start playing like this."

"Ain't nobody playing, Kenyon. I'm sick of him and his lack of consideration for the rest of us," Dee snapped.

"Lack of consideration? You foolin'! I been getting it out the mud since I was sixteen- for all of us. Everything I've ever done has been for this fucking family. I put yo nigga in a position so that he could feed ya'll! What is you saying?"

"Hermano, por favor deje de," I demanded.

"Esta mierdo esta hecho," Juan screamed before leaving the room.

"Next time I tell you to shut your fucking mouth, I expect you to do just that. This shit is uncalled for. Whether you want to own it or not, Rochelle responsible for this shit too. That nigga ain't hold a gun to her head. Yes, we put y'all in this shit. But it's on yall to know when to ride and when to ride off. You and G always follow instructions and aint shit ever happen. Rochelle took the wrong route, she was speeding, and she had a strap on her. They searched the car because they seen the gun under the seat. This nigga can be selfish, but he went all in to make sure she get out of this. You out of order! Start acting like you're my fucking wife."

Kenyon walked out and slammed the door. Within seconds Dee had her face buried in the pillow sobbing uncontrollably. I didn't know what to do. I just wrapped my arms around her, laid my head on her shoulder and cried with her.

Fifty

"Meet me at the warehouse," Juan ended the call.

When Kenyon arrived he found Juan sitting on a bench inside of the warehouse. Surprisingly, he was an emotional mess. His face looked like he had been crying.

"Yo Uno what the hell going on?"

"Pimp gone!"

Kenyon was confused, "What do you mean Pimp gone?"

"A few days ago I got up with the homie. He was trying to get right so I got him together. For real, I had just copped some more dirty from Ms. Carol. I gave him all that I had just to show love. I get a call like 'Pimp overdosed on lean in his sleep. My patna died and I served him the shit that killed him."

"Damn! I told Pimp to slow up on that drank."

"What's crazy is we had the illest rap when I saw him. We talked about you, Bun, our old ladies and just life period. He told me no matter what, you always take care of family. I was tight about the way Dee came at me. I aint gone lie. That nigga helped me get a better understanding of the whole situation. We agreed to link sometime next week. I told him I wanted to play with that music shit and see what I could do," Juan explained.

"Tomorrow not promised. I can't lie this one got me tight! I know Bun probably done. This whole situation reminds me of Marcus. Everyday I think about that nigga and where we went wrong with Memphis."

Juan looked Kenyon in the eyes, " All I ever had in this world was y'all. My people was all fucked up. This shit real. I don't think I can take no more losses, K."

"Bro we don't have to take no more if we get out of this shit. Now is the time, Uno. Trust me on this, man."

Kenyon had never discussed with Juan what he had found out when he went through Officer Winston's files. When they popped Dave, he informed them that Uno was his plug. He gave them the shop's address and told them where their trap house was. What Kenyon found surprising was they had Juan listed under the aliases "Uno" and "AK." Nobody referred to Juan as AK. Actually, that was Kenyon's alias for doing business in Memphis. Kenyon started putting two and two together and recalled Tone and David being cool until he started hanging with Marcus.

Once Kenyon thought about it, he knew that Dave was involved in Marcus's murder. Tone didn't have the heart to kill Marcus on his own. Dave had always been envious of their crew, so Kenyon knew it was an ideal move for him. Since Dave had been released, nobody in the hood had seen him. Kenyon knew that once Uno got wind of Dave's involvement, he would kill him. With everything going on, Kenyon knew they did not need the extra heat.

He decided to wait a few days before speaking to Juan since he was grieving Pimp's death. In the meantime he knew that he needed a plan to take care of the situation. Pondering on the right move on his drive home, Kenyon knew he had to be calculated.

"Bae," Kenyon called for Denise when he got in the house.

"Kenyon, I'm upstairs," she yelled.

He ran up stairs and Dee was playing music as she braided Amire's hair.

"Daddy!" she screamed.

"What's up, baby?" he responded kissing her forehead.

Amire giggled, "Mommy braiding my hair. She said I'm gone be fly."

Kenyon responded, "I see, Baby. It looks beautiful."

"My-My, go tell your brother to clean his room and run the dishwasher."

"Yes ma'am," Amire responded before running down the steps.

Kenyon grabbed Denise's hand, "Bae, I got some bad news. Pimp died today."

"I seen it on the news. December 4th is a bad day. You know it's my dad's death anniversary as well. Too close to the holidays."

"Juan was jacked up earlier. He had just seen him too."

Denise joked, "His ass probably the one that sold him the lean. They said he overdosed in the hotel."

Kenyon shook his head, "Man…"

"Wow!"

"Well today I need you to be cool. I invited everybody over so we can just have family time. G making rice and I'm gone grill some meat. I just need you to get some side dishes together if you don't mind."

"Husband, I worked last night. Don't you think you should've asked me before you decided to have a family reunion?"

"No foul, Bae. It was last minute. After talking to Uno, I knew that we all really needed to be together, surrounded by love. Feel me?"

Denise smirked, "I understand. You get on my nerves, but that's the reason why I love you. I'm gone have to take a nap first though. When you go downstairs tell Amire to come get her hair finished."

"Anything else, Boss?" Kenyon joked.

"Yup! I'm missing that mouth of yours. Kitty needs the talk today."

"You a cold piece of work, Ma. I got you though. Tonight I'm gone tear that muthafucka out the frame."

Fifty-One

"Good Morning, Rochelle. How are you today?"

"Jeff, I am not okay. This is a nightmare!"

The lawyer grabbed Rochelle's folder and his iPad. "So, I'm just going to be straight up with you. We don't really have much of a defense unless you were under someone's direct orders in fear for your life. The good thing is, they don't want you; they want information. Otherwise, she's gonna keep playing hardball."

"What am I looking at?"

"She sent this over," Jeff handed Rochelle a plea bargain. "They really want to know where the drugs came from. She knows you aren't the dealer. They believe that it's someone you're connected to. If you give them that information, you can walk away without a scratch."

Rochelle broke down, "Jeff, I can't snitch. It's not in my blood to do. My life would be over and our safety would be in jeopardy. This is a cold game."

"I understand the consequences of getting tangled up with the wrong people. Dallas is the stomping grounds for the Emel Cartel. Those guys are very dangerous."

"What can we do with what we have?"

"The best I can do is try to get you out of the double digits with this being your first offense. I can bluff and see what we come up with. Now, there is a witness that's being concealed for safety. I have no clue what this has to do with your case, but I will know more at our next hearing."

Rochelle understood that she was going to have to do some time. She did not want to leave her son, but she knew that there was no other option. When she left the lawyer's office, she decided to go talk to Dee and Kenyon. They always gave her good advice and she wanted to know if they would be willing to care for Juan while she was away.

When she arrived at the house, I was there with the kids. We had just finished taking family pictures.

"Hey, Ro!"

"Hey, Geezy. How did my baby do? I missed him."

I smiled, "He did really good. Your niece was the problem for real."

Rochelle grabbed Baby Juan out of his seat and held him. I walked into the kitchen to give them some bonding time. After almost twenty minutes, we heard Rochelle wailing from the living room.

"What the fuck have I done," she screamed. "I'm going to prison and leaving my son! GOD, what have I done?"

Denise became emotional as well. "What did the lawyer say, Ro?" she asked in a somber tone.

"Basically, I don't have no defense. They have some witness and the arrest was clean. The prosecutor is willing to cut a deal if I snitch. She wants to know where the dope came from in Dallas."

"Did you holla at Uno? He might have a play for you."

"Griselda, your brother thinks everything is a joke. He has his mind made up of me going to trial. This fool thinks he can bribe the jury."

I became annoyed after hearing that, "In Texas? He sound so damn stupid."

"Right," Dee chimed in.

"He told me he was working on something for me, but time is running out. We don't even know who this mystery witness is or nothing about it. Jeff gone try to work out a deal for me under ten years. Right now he said that's the best he can do."

Rochelle's news had us all in shambles. That night we all cried and loved on each other. None of us really knew how crazy life would be dealing with street niggas. Funny thing is we didn't know anything else but the streets.

Denise put on some music to lighten the mood. We were H-Walking to "Walk it Out" by DJ Unk when Kenyon walked in.

"Ya'll so ratchet," he joked.

"Don't hate," Dee snapped while in the middle of a dance move.

Kenyon did a little two-step as he headed towards the steps, "I would jam on yall, but a brother is tired."

"I'll be right back y'all," Dee said as she followed Kenyon up the stairs.

"Girl, bye. You ain't coming back. It's cool though. I got my other sister," Rochelle stated.

While waiting on Kenyon to get out of the shower, Denise fell asleep on the bed. For a few minutes Kenyon watched her in adoration before waking her up.

"Dee," he spoke softly.

She opened one eye, "What, Kenyon?"

"I gotta tell you something."

"Tell me later. I'm sleep," she whined.

Kenyon grabbed her arm, "Mrs. Green, wake yo ass up! I got into school."

"School?" she mumbled.

"Sit up real quick," he directed.

Denise sat up still trying to break her sleep. "This better be good, negro. I am exhausted."

"Bae, I been doing a lot of studying. I reached out to a college and they said I needed some ACT test score to get in the business program. I grabbed the books and took the test last month. They sent my results today and I got a 25. Dee, that's gone get me into college."

"Kenyon, why didn't you tell me?"

"There are certain things a man has to do on his own. I gave you my word and I meant it. I just had to go about it my own way. As my wife, I just need you to trust me and support me throughout the process. Our new life is on the way. I promise. I just gotta help clean up this mess we made first."

Part Six

Fifty-Two

A few months had passed and everybody had been laying low. Kenyon was occupied applying to colleges in Georgia and creating his business plan. Meanwhile Juan focused on keeping Rochelle calm and finding a new spot to set up shop. Because they hadn't been in Sunnyside, the hood assumed they were gone for good.

"Aye, ain't nobody seen them squad niggas?"

Dave bragged, " Man, I sent them niggas packing. That nigga Uno might be a shooter, but he scared of the joint."

Kevin wasn't feeling Dave's vibe. "Bro you better be careful fucking with them niggas. Shit, you seen how they body rocked Young Tone."

"I ain't worried about shit. The feds on them niggas now. Sunnyside is mine! I'm bout to change the game out chea'. That nigga Uno ain't got shit coming and that's real talk."

"Just be careful out here, D," he warned.

Dave was one of those guys that enjoyed partying. When he left the spot, he decided to go to Joe's Bar. He was well known so people showed him a lot of love when he walked through the door. The bartender stopped what she was doing and brought a bottle of Hennessy to his table. He took a few sips, popped his Percocets and looked around to see what hoe he could take home.

"Hi Dave," Tiona said as she approached his table.

"What yo young ass doing in here?" he questioned.

"I'm legal now so Joe said I could come in. You know I turned eighteen last week."

Dave looked Tiona's body up and down. "I see you looking good though. Where yo nigga?"

"I'm single," she bragged rubbing her ass against his arm.

"You might as well come fuck with a real nigga. I may be too much for you though."

Tiona rolled her eyes, "Nigga please! Don't let my age fool you. I'm really about that life."

At that moment R. Kelly's 'I'm a Flirt' came on and Tiona started dancing in front of Dave. He watched in admiration as she swayed her hips and popped her ass. Dave wanted Tiona and he knew that she would be down. Within a few minutes he whispered in her ear and they were exiting the bar. When they got into the car, they began kissing passionately. Dave had managed to pull off Tiona's panties while he played with her young pussy.

Dave didn't believe in taking women to his house, so he decided to pull up to his homie's house a few blocks over. When they arrived, Tiona immediately pulled his dick out and started sucking it. Dave turned his headlights off, reclined the seat and rubbed her head as he moaned.

Before he could bust a nut, Tee quickly removed her dress and hopped on his dick. After a few strokes she found her rhythm and bounced as Dave sucked her titties. Tiona pulled Dave as she tried to stretch out to the passenger seat.

"Oh shit!" she screamed noticing a man in all black standing outside of Dave's door.

Within moments Tiona was drug from where she laid, out of the passenger door. "Be quiet," the other assailant demanded as he laid her faced down on the grass. She was so focused on the man she saw, she didn't realize there was someone else on her side of the truck.

Face down, Tiona heard what sounded like splashes of water or lasers as she later described. She knew that Dave had been shot. Afraid that she would be next, she laid still. When she could no longer hear the footprints or body movements of the men, she cried out for help.

"Help," she screamed repeatedly. Finally, a man came running out of the house they were stopped in front of. As soon as he seen Dave's body, he spazzed out.

"Not my Patna, mane! Come on, D," he panted. Tiona was on the grass naked on her knees and he instructed her to find her clothes while he ran into the house to call the police.

When the emergency squad arrived, they pronounced Dave dead at the scene. They put Tiona in the back of another ambulance vehicle so that she could be assessed and questioned.

"Ma'am can you tell us what happened?" the detective asked.

"We were having sex in the car and two people in all black walked up. One of them pulled me out the passenger door and put me on the ground. They told me to be quiet and all I heard were laser sounds. I knew they had shot Dave. After I didn't hear them anymore, I started screaming for help. That's when Steve came out the house and we called you."

Dave's family had arrived on the scene. "Let me find out that bitch had something to do with this shit," she heard his cousin say.

"I'm scared. I did not have anything to do with this. If people think I did somebody is going to hurt me," she pleaded to the officers.

"Are you sure there's not anything else we need to know," he asked.

"No. I told you everything. We literally just had left Joe's Bar."

The detective instructed one of the officers to go to the bar to see if there was any footage and if anybody could verify Tiona's story.

Fifty-Three

As soon as he left Tiffany's house, he contacted the detectives he had been working with. He told them everything Rochelle had informed Tiffany of that day. By the time Rochelle left Dallas, there were already units in place following her. Luckily, Manuel always had a sting in place whenever they were moving dope. Rochelle actually picked the drugs up from a park in the heart of Dallas. The package was right where they informed her it would be. She looked around to make sure no one was watching and proceeded with putting the drugs into the car. Before getting back on the road, she stopped at a local gas station and stored the drugs as Juan had instructed.

The detectives caught everything on camera and therefore had Rochelle with the possession far before she started speeding. Their case was solid, but without the witness that directed them to her, things got complicated.

Jeff approached us outside the courtroom, "Good news ladies, Rochelle has accepted a deal. She's gonna have to do five years in a federal facility and also a mandatory eight years on parole. The great thing is she will be close to home, a few hours away in Bryan. The facility offers programs and incentives for mothers and good behavior. Since she does not have a violent offense, she should do well there."

"Hallelujah!" their mom shouted while throwing her hands in the air.

Denise shook Jeff's hand, "Thank you so much for all that you've done, Jeff."

"No need to thank me. You should be thanking the killer of their informant. That's what gave us the leverage to negotiate."

I couldn't believe that Dave's murder changed Rochelle's case. The streets were talking and there were so many stories circulating. Some people were saying that Juan had him killed and others were saying that Little Tiona set him up. Nobody knew for sure and since they didn't rob him, the story about Juan held more weight. I didn't believe my brother was the killer though. Juan would never leave a living witness. That's not how he moved. If he was going to kill someone, everybody involved would have died.

"I'm sorry to hear that someone died, but I am happy that my sister does not have to spend the rest of her life in jail," Denise explained.

Jeff responded, "As long as she stays out of trouble and is back here to report on time, everything will be fine. Just make sure she keeps a low profile because they are watching her. The DA knows Rochelle was not acting alone and she wants to know where the drugs came from. She's very determined to take everyone down."

We knew that meant Rochelle needed to be as far away from us as possible. The good thing is the Feds gave her some time before she had to report, which gave us time to plan. Denise and I waited around for her to be released by the Judge before we headed back to the hotel room.

Juan and Kenyon were there with the kids. They wanted to show their support, but knew that they could not physically be in the courtroom. I'm sure they already had profiled Denise and I off rip.

"Daddy daycare," I joked walking through the door.

"Estos ninos estan locos," Juan replied.

"Don't be calling our babies crazy," I snapped.

Kenyon interrupted, "I don't know about crazy, but they sure wore us the hell out. Anyway, how did everything go?"

"I took a deal," Rochelle explained.

"Deal?" Juan asked.

"I gotta do five years with the Feds. They also gave me eight years of probation. I was looking at twenty for all of the dope, but their witness got killed. Y'all know who I think the witness was?"

"Dave," I replied.

"Hell yeah!" she exclaimed.

Juan looked at us, "Everybody think I body rocked that hoe ass nigga. This time it wasn't me though. Shit, I can only think that the universe came through for you, Ro."

Denise snapped, "So, apparently all of y'all okay with my sister going to jail?"

"Dee, don't start please! I'm just happy that I don't have to spend the rest of my life in jail for this shit. I can do the five years and move on with my life. That's what I want to focus on."

"Listen this is a fucked up situation for us all, ya dig? Nobody wins when one of us has to go away. Yes, Ro gotta do some time, but she gone be alright. We got her back and we gone hold her down. Now we just gotta tighten up and make sure our shit in order. We don't need no division or negativity right now," Kenyon stated.

Juan and I were silent. We both knew Denise blamed Juan for Rochelle being caught. It hurt me, but Juan didn't care. He knew that this came with the game. Truthfully, I think he was more intrigued by the fact that Rochelle stayed solid. That solidified their bond in his eyes. Manuel and the connect were also happy to learn that our crew was solid. Juan knew that they would trust him more, which meant bigger business.

Kenyon was a thinker so we never knew how he really felt. What I did know was Rochelle, Dee, and I were in pain. Unable to voice it, we suffered in silence. All of us had been involved in the operation in some fashion. At any point either of us could've been next and that was a fear that we couldn't shake.

Fifty-Four

"Hey beautiful," Rome greeted me.

Mari interrupted, "Hi!"

"Go play girl and stay out of grown folks business," I demanded. That child was something else.

Rome wiped his head with a white towel, "It's hot as hell out here, yo. This Texas heat ain't no joke."

"It's not that bad today. Wait until it hits like one-twenty. That's gone really give you a taste of Texas for sure. Anyway, what you doing here?"

"I just wanted to catch up. It seems like I'm not good enough for your time these days."

I smirked, "That's not true. I've been extremely busy with everything. So my bad about being unavailable."

"So that means you're still not ready to answer my question I'm assuming."

"Rome, I haven't been in a relationship since Marcus. I don't even know if I even know how to be somebody's girlfriend. I really like you, but I just don't know."

"Well I tell you what, you got some time to figure out what you want. I can't promise I'll be here forever, but I do understand your situation."

Denise walked up as he was talking. It was her day to do the paperwork at the center. "Hey ya'll," she chimed in.

"Hey," we responded collectively.

"I'm gonna bounce. Get at me when you figure things out," he stated before walking away.

"What's going on with y'all?" Dee asked.

I rolled my eyes, "He wants to be with me in a relationship. He's been calling and texting and I have been dodging him."

"Why? I thought you liked him?"

"I do but I'm not sure about no relationship. I low key feel like my life is all over the place since Rochelle took this deal. I don't know whether I'm coming or going."

Denise was confused, "What do you mean?"

"I'm scared, Dee. I don't know if these people are watching us. Juan acts like its no big deal. Kenyon is chill as hell. You're mad all the time. Things just seem really off with everybody. A relationship is the least of my worries at this point."

"Honestly, it's been crazy for me as well. I never wanted any of us to get hurt or to take these kind of losses, but that comes with the game. We're getting older now and we have these kids to worry about. Like I told K, it's time for us all to do something different. I'm tired of the shit all together."

"Actually, I'm ready to leave Texas now more than ever."

"Have y'all made a decision about when yall want to leave?"

"Kenyon wants to go to Atlanta. He said that's where he wants to go to school. It's cheaper than Cali and of course we have business there. So we should be figuring things out within the next few months. Just be ready to pack your shit."

I laughed, "Girl, I cannot leave my brother and nephew!"

"Baby Uno is going wherever we go, okay? Plus, Juan will leave if you and the kids are no longer here. Trust me! Y'all are all that this fool cares about. Now, I don't know if he'd still do business in Texas, but he definitely wouldn't live here."

"Maybe that's the only way I can help save him, huh?"

"Maybe."

Fifty-Five

"Bae, did you go to the fish market yet? Mommy said she wanted to have salmon."

Kenyon was busy seasoning the meat. "Naw, but we gone do this fish last. Uno can stop and get it. Text him and tell him to grab some salmon, catfish and Old Bay seasoning."

"Okay. I'm going to take a quick nap. Today, I'm really not feeling well."

"Dee, you've been doing a lot with work and the kids and shit. It's time for you to let your body rest a while. Maybe take some time off or something."

"I made a doctor's appointment to make sure there's nothing else going on. For the most part, I'm just tired and my body aches."

"Go get in the bed. I'll finish up in here until Griselda comes to help me. We got this," he stated before slapping Dee's ass.

When I arrived at their home, Dee was in bed and Kenyon was in the kitchen. He was running back and forth from the back yard checking on the meat he was grilling. There were greens and gumbo cooking on the stove.

"It smells good in this joint!" I yelled.

"You already know how I do," Kenyon bragged.

"Well I have the arroz con pollo and the strawberry poke cake."

Kenyon grabbed the items out of my hand and put them on the counter where he had the food laid out.

"Sis, you think you can help me finish these sides? Dee still in the bed. She's not feeling well."

"I got you. Throw some UGK on though so I can vibe out," I stated while washing my hands.

For the next few hours, Kenyon and I cooked the rest of the food. We listened to music and cracked jokes the entire time. Dee's family members had started to arrive while we were finishing up.

Dee finally woke up and made it down stairs. She finished setting everything up while I cleaned the kitchen and Kenyon showered.

"Thanks for helping, G. I needed that rest."

"Already! I'll be back though. I have to go help Uno get the baby out of the car."

Juan had arrived with the baby and I couldn't wait to see them. When I walked in the door with him, Dee's family rushed me and took the baby. They hadn't seen him much since Rochelle had been locked up.

"What y'all feeding this baby?" Dee's Aunt Jane asked.

"That's Dee giving him all of those chicken bones and potatoes," I joked.

Juan greeted everybody and I noticed that their brother Junior didn't speak. I knew that some of them didn't like Juan because Rochelle was in jail, but they never stepped to him with any drama. Although Junior didn't say anything, I knew that he felt some type of way and I wasn't feeling his energy. I had planned on saying something to him, but I decided to chill and just enjoy the cookout.

Kenyon set up the table in the back where all of the men were playing dominoes. I made margaritas and the ladies drank while we listened to music. Everyone seemed to be having a good time until we heard yelling from the backyard.

"If you got something to say, nigga, say it!" Juan yelled.

Kenyon put his hand in front of Juan's chest, "Uno, chill out. This shit ain't about nothing!"

"Nigga fuck you! I do got something to say. You're the reason my sister is in fuckin prison. What kind of man let's the mother of their child go to the joint? But you a real nigga right?" Junior yelled sarcastically.

The next thing I knew, Juan had picked up the bottle of liquor and cracked Junior over the head with it. Blood splattered from his forehead as he stumbled out of the chair. He tried to stand up, but Juan had already made his way to him. Juan stomped Junior several times while Kenyon and the others tried to grab him. When Juan got mad, he became a maniac.

"¡Detene Hermano!" I yelled several times before Juan finally stopped fighting them off.

"What the fuck is going on with you fools?" Dee yelled.

"Ladies, go back in the house. Let us handle this shit. Please," Kenyon asked.

When we got into the house, I noticed Junior's wife in the corner on the phone.

"Marie, who are you calling?" I asked.

"The police! Your brother is an animal!" she screamed.

Before I knew it, I had lunged at her and punched her in the face. Now I wasn't much of a fighter. I didn't go around starting drama with people. However, I was all about my family and I did not believe in calling the police about anything. The last thing we needed was Juan catching a case.

Marie tried to swing back and ended up scratching my face. When I saw blood, I completely lost it.

"Stupid bitch," I yelled before tackling her to the ground. She pulled my hair while I punched her in the face. We didn't fight long because Dee and her Aunt pulled me off of her.

Kenyon grabbed me and carried me out of the house. I was not finished with that puta! He made Juan and I leave before the police arrived. When we were pulling out of the complex, we passed two squad cars pulling in.

"Damn, you see that?" I asked.

"Kenyon better handle this shit before I have to fuck up Dee's people. Last thing I need to worry about right now is twelve. Ain't no telling what these fuck niggas gone yap about."

I felt Juan wholeheartedly. "We definitely gotta make sure they don't talk. I'm gone tell Ken to meet us at the spot to see what they told the pigs."

Fifty-Six

"Buenos Dias."

"Que hora es," I replied opening the door for Juan.

"Shit I don't know. It's time to get up though."

Juan rarely showed up unannounced, which made me nervous. "Que pasa?"

"I got a move for you."

"Move? Now you know it's hot right now. I don't want no parts in the game right now, Uno."

"Look…You know I'd never put you in harms way! I never have and I never will. Rochelle got caught on some fool shit."

I wasn't feeling it. "Juan, we got enough paper to chill right now. I'm not trying to get caught up."

"I don't have anybody else I can trust. Dee got Ken all scared. Shit gotta get back moving. Ya'll gotta stop acting so pussy."

"Ain't nobody acting pussy. We're acting smart. We got fuckin kids to think about. You know how I feel about this."

Juan clapped his hands slowly, "Hermana, that's exactly why we need this move! It'll be life changing. Plus, I gotta make back what I put out for Rochelle."

I understood that Rochelle going to jail was a major hit for Juan. That's my brother and having his back wasn't even questionable. However, I just couldn't shake the anxiety I had about making another move. Just as I was about to express my concern, the doorbell rang.

"Who's there?" I mumbled. Juan beat me to the door and opened it.

Juan opened the door and looked Rome directly in the eyes.

"Hi, I'm Rome...is Griselda here?"

"G!" Juan yelled as if he didn't know I was on the other side of the wall.

"Let him in," I responded.

Juan backed up and Rome walked in. I could tell that he was slightly uncomfortable with my brother being in the house.

"Introduce yourself," Juan demanded.

"Juan," I yelled.

"It's cool." Rome interrupted. "I'm Rome, a good friend of Griselda's."

"We don't have friends around here. It's only family, feel me? So what you looking for?"

I put my hand up in front of Juan, "You don't have to answer that Rome. Juan was just leaving."

Last thing I needed was Juan busting Rome's ass in my house. I ended that conversation quickly.

Juan kissed me on my forehead and said, "Maltratare' a alguien sobre ti."

My brother's words were firm. I knew that he really would kill anybody who messed me over.

When Juan walked out the door, I apologized to Rome for his behavior. Juan could be very disrespectful at times. The last thing I wanted was Rome feeling like Juan was challenging his manhood.

"I'm really not tripping. Your people don't know me. They are supposed to be overprotective. I would feel uncomfortable if they weren't. I heard about your brother and I am not trying to go there with him. All a nigga trying to do is make you his lady feel me?"

"I hear you! Now, lets see what you do. We both know a pair of lips can say anything."

Rome pulled me close to him, "As long as you're willing to let me show you we Gucci."

Fifty-Seven

Since Rochelle had been locked up, I had not been to a visit. Honestly, I thought that it was bad luck going to the prison. However, it was her birthday and she requested that we all come visit. Their family members decided that they did not want to visit with us, so they went earlier in the week. There was still tension from the fight.

So that we could be comfortable, Juan had me book a small family van. We decided that this time we would take all of the kids. Oddly, Kenyon decided not to come with us at the last minute, but sent his love.

Camp Bryan, where she was locked up, was about two and a half hours away from Sunnyside. Dee reserved a hotel room where we could go clean up before our visit.

"For some odd reason, I am so damn tired," I complained.

"You better get some energy. We have a long day ahead of us," Dee instructed.

Juan was taking forever in the bathroom. "We gone be late messing with Juan's ass."

"Hurry up, Shitty," Dee yelled at the bathroom door.

About ten minutes later, Juan came out of the bathroom dressed in his pajamas.

"What are you doing?" I asked.

"I'm bout to take a nap. What you doing," he responded sarcastically.

"Don't start acting silly. I'm going to see Rochelle. You know the reason why we're here?"

Dee stormed into the bathroom. I could tell she was irritated with Juan and so was I.

"Juan, you can't back out on us now. You know she wanted to see you too."

"Fuck Rochelle! She said some foul shit to me this morning so I'm not going. I'm gone show her ass what it's like to do time without me."

"Stop being childish! That shit is small. Its her birthday, Uno. The least you could do was show up regardless of what was said. Ro proved her loyalty to you and you gotta do the same flatout."

"I just told yo goofy ass I wasn't going. I got y'all here. Take the baby and go have a good time."

At first I thought Juan was being funny, but he wasn't. Dee and I finally said forget it and loaded the kids in the van. We rode in silence, studying the scenery. I noticed corn stalks and tomatoes in one field. As we got closer to the facility, there were a lot of barbed wire fences, like you see on movies. The building where we were going was bricked and had yellow vinyl.

When we got in, it smelt like something died. Dee said she smelt piss and boiled eggs. The other visitors seemed to be comfortable in the environment, but I was tripping at how filthy it was. I even saw a roach crawling on the wall where they were scanning the ID cards.

It took us about twenty minutes to get checked in before the guard escorted us to our visiting quarters. They provided us with juice and cookies, which seemed odd. We were seated on a bench, which resembled those in the parks. Rochelle ran up to the table in tears when she noticed us.

"Geezy!" she yelled hugging me tightly.

"Teedy!" all of the kids yelled before hugging her.

Dee handed Uno to her last and she just cried as she held her son.

We were emotional as well.

"You looking good, Pooh," Dee stated rubbing Rochelle's back.

"Thanks, Sis! What's up with y'all? How is everybody?"

"Everybody is good girl. It's so good to see you. I really missed you, Sister. Sorry I didn't come sooner."

Rochelle grabbed my hand, "It's okay. I understand. I'm just thankful for all that y'all do for my baby. He look so good man."

"He's identical to Uno when he was a baby."

"Speaking of your brother, I thought he was coming too?" Rochelle asked.

Dee rolled her eyes, "He's here at the hotel. He drove us down here, but decided not to come for whatever reason."

"Because he's selfish! Don't even get me started on that asshole."

The kids went to the next table and started playing a board game. That gave us time to talk.

I wanted to know what happened between them, "What did he do?"

"So earlier I call him just to make sure y'all were still coming. This muthafucka ask me why I keep on calling. He kind of caught me off guard, so I'm like what do you mean why am I calling? He proceeds to tell me that he's grown and knows where he supposed to be and when. So we got into it. I rarely argue with Uno, but I'm sick of his shit straight up."

"He really annoys me acting like he's so emotionally unavailable. I love my brother, but he acts stupid as hell sometime."

I could tell Dee was trying to refrain from going there, but she couldn't hold her composure. "G, you're going to have to excuse me, but I'm sick of this shit. Girl, you then gave up your whole life for this nigga, damn near. You're in jail and away from your child. Now, you're a convicted felon and this nigga don't have the decency to even show up on your birthday. At some point, Ro, you gotta see shit for what it is. That man is not for you- period. We all love Juan, but we also know that he does him. I can't continue to see you hurting behind this nothing ass nigga because he's the baby's father. At the end of the day, let him be a dad, do your time and fuck him."

"I agree with Dee. At the end of the day relationships go both ways. If he's not doing you right then bounce on his ass. He will see in the end that he messed up."

"He does provide for me. I don't go without nothing in here. He takes care of the baby and that's really my biggest concern. Jail gets lonely, y'all. I miss having that intimacy with a man. So yeah I call him because I love him and I still planned on building with him. Honestly, I think that since he knows I ain't snitch, he's done with me. Like he threw me the money and bounced."

Dee was firm, "That's what the fuck it is. You're still young and poppin'. Get on MySpace or Facebook and find you somebody else. Juan is not the only man out there."

"That's easy for you to say, Dee, Kenyon then had you on lock for years. Mommy got sick of chasing that fool off so she finally just let y'all be."

"Trust me if he don't make some changes I'm bouncing on his ass too. I got my career and these kids to worry about. I can't take what all comes along with the game too much longer. This shit is exhausting."

I nodded in agreement. "It's just too much altogether."

"Well at least we have each other. Y'all know these niggas love the streets. They gone do what they do regardless. We just have to continue to stick together and make sure we get out of this shit. I don't want y'all to end up like me. This jail shit is for the birds. If I could go back, I would have never ran that dope for Uno. He would've just had to find somebody else. It's so many chicks in here for their niggas or family members who leave them for dead. I thought my situation was different, but I guess not. Y'all just gotta promise me that y'all won't get caught up in this shit."

Dee and I felt Rochelle's pain. We promised that we would always stick together and leave the bullshit behind us. Even if that meant leaving the men we loved the most.

Fifty-Eight

As it got closer to the holiday season both Kenyon and Juan seemed to be focused on the money. Kenyon had started a small landscaping business and hired a few of the neighborhood kids to help him. They went to the suburbs and planted flowers, cut grass and did lawn care. Our lawn at the center looked great because of their hard work.

Juan's business appeared to be the same old flow. He had been back and forth to Dallas dealing with Manuel. Despite our concerns, Juan decided that he wasn't going to let anything get in the way of him getting his money.

One day Kenyon was working at the center when Juan rolled up. "What's good, Bro?"

"I can't call it. I see you out here slaving," Juan joked.

"Slaving huh? Naw, I'm getting my shit together. You know what I'm on. What's up with you though? I know you ain't here to take a nigga to lunch."

Juan got out of his Lexus and grabbed a shovel. "I got a power move lined up for us," he whispered to Kenyon.

"What you mean by power move?"

"My primo in Dallas got a connect in Denver. I'm talking bout warehouses full of everything the streets need. From dirty to straight drop! They told me like 'come shop.' Niggas don't gotta do shit but get the weight and sell it."

"I'm good."

"Ken, bro I need you. This is the move that's gone change our lives. We comfortable right now. This type of weight gone pay for the kids' college. I figured we could move it ourselves until we found some solid little niggas to move it for us. For real, I'm only trying to sell weight. Once we make a few trips, we can bow out and go do our thang."

Kenyon thought about Juan's proposal. "Let me sleep on it. You know it's so many moving pieces. I need time to analyze everything. In the meantime, find out everything you can about their operation. I think I got an idea of somebody that can help you move that shit, but I gotta check a few things out first."

"Already," Juan exclaimed.

"Bro, I'm not saying yes and I'm not saying no. What I can promise though is I'll never leave you out here to dry. I'm gone make sure you alright, Uno. No matter what."

"I already know."

After Juan left, Kenyon packed his truck up and headed home. When he got there, he noticed that Dee left him a note on the refrigerator to check the mail in the drawer. After heating up his dinner, Kenyon opened a letter he received from Clark Atlanta University. Kenyon sat in shock as he read that he had been accepted into college. He was finally on his way to receiving the business degree he'd always dreamed of. All he had to do was figure out how he could balance the streets, his family and now his education.

Fifty-Nine

"Hermana, can you meet me a el punto?" Juan asked.

"Yo tengo los ninos."

"Duh! I forgot you had the kids. I thought they were with K.Dot. Damn! Alright, gimme a second I'm bout to fall through."

Juan hung up the phone and about thirty minutes later, he was standing in my kitchen. He played with the kids for a minute and put cartoons on to occupy them while we talked.

"Why you looking like that?"

I gave Juan a smirk, "What's this all about? I know you're not here just because you love us."

"I'm doing some business with Manuel. Some packages are gonna be shipped from out the way. I need you to grab them."

"Uno, you know Vlad told us to never do business by mail. What are you thinking?" I questioned.

"Chill! I got this. All I need you to do is grab the boxes and take them to the spot when you get them. I'll be the one sending them so everything should be smooth ya hear me?"

I really didn't want to be a part of the move, "I guess."

"No mierda! I need you. Everything is going to be cool. You always follow directions and use your head. This time is no different, Griselda."

Of course I agreed to help my brother. I was stern about my reservations, but in the end my loyalty triumphed my fear. He assured me that I would be straight and I had to trust that. Juan let me know that the moves he was making were going to get us out the game for good. That made me happy because I wanted nothing more than to be out of the game. To clear my mind, I decided to take the kids to Dee and go to dinner with Rome.

Rome came into the restaurant with roses and a few balloons. He greeted me with a kiss, which made me happy. "Hello, Beautiful," he stated.

"Hey, handsome," I smiled back.

We ordered cocktails and caught up with one another. Then we got on the subject of the holidays and the conversation shifted.

"So, G, I was thinking that we could spend Thanksgiving together at my mom's. I'd like for you to bring the kids so we can all get acquainted."

Initially, I was shocked. The last thing I expected was for Rome to invite the kids to Georgia. We had only been together for a short time. "I'll let you know. We typically go on vacation or do something as a family for the holidays. I've never spent one without my brother for real."

"I understand. Just tell me that you'll at least consider it. My folks would love to meet Mari. I told my mom all about her."

"Is that her calling you now?" I asked sarcastically.

Rome was caught off guard, "Nah. That's probably just a bill collector or something."

"Well I have to use the restroom. Make sure the bill collector ain't calling when I get back."

When I came out the restroom, I noticed someone at the table talking to Rome. I knew that it wasn't a waitress so I was immediately thrown off. As I got closer to the table, I realized that it was Lil. Britt was coming in the door behind her. I rushed to the table so fast, I almost fell in my Jimmy Choo's.

"What the fuck is going on?" I yelled.

"This clown ass nigga denying my child. That's what's going on!" Lillian yelled.

Rome looked at Britt, "Yo, how the fuck y'all find me man?"

"I've been following yo ass nigga. You won't answer none of my calls. So what you thought I was just about to let this shit go!"

Britt grabbed her best friend's arm, "Let's go please! I told you we would handle this shit at another time, Lillian, damn."

All of the restaurant patrons were staring at us and I was extremely embarrassed. Lil's behavior reminded me of Bianca and I wanted nothing more than to get my stuff and get out of there. I couldn't even look at Rome.

"This is too much," I stated snatching my purse and walking out of the door.

I heard Rome yelling from the parking lot, "Bitch, you're out of line. I don't ever disrespect women, but you're pushing me to the limit! I told you I'm not that baby's father. You think I am, then run me a test. Other than that, we don't have shit to talk about. Now, you following me and shit, showing up on a nigga! Nah. I aint about that madness. If you call me again or show up anywhere I am, I will put yo ratchet ass in jail."

Lillian threw a glass of water on Rome. I didn't want to talk to either of them so I got in my car and skirted out of there. Under no circumstance was I dealing with some baby mama drama again.

Sixty

"Go to 615 North Lawry. Be there by seven sharp. Regular move," Juan instructed before hanging up the phone.

As directed I made the move. When I got to the location, the packages were already there on the porch. I noticed some white people outside across the street. I decided to park the loaner and walk to get the boxes. I was dressed in costume. Normally, I wore all black, but this time I was extra cautious. I had on a construction outfit and I was dressed like a man. I pretended to scan the box as if it was my equipment to throw off the onlookers. When they were not paying me any attention, I grabbed the box and rushed off the block. Normally, I would've got back in the loaner, but this time I decided to leave it. There was a bus stop on the next corner, so I decided to catch the bus to blend in with the working people. I didn't want to worry Juan so I texted one of the homies to pick up the car. After I got off the bus in Sunnyside, I tried to reach Juan, but he didn't answer. So as a last resort, I called Kenyon.

"Yo?" he answered.

"Squad up," I instructed.

"Say no more," Kenyon stated before hanging up the call.

Forty minutes later Kenyon arrived at the spot. He checked everything to make sure the building was secure. He pulled the landscaping truck into the garage and I gave him the boxes. Kenyon decided to store the work in the safe; inside of the chandelier. "You ready to talk?" he asked.

"Uno told me to go pick up the packages. I was feeling uncomfortable about the scene so I left the beater and told Quis to go get it. I took the bus all the way to the hood before I called you. I've been blowing this nigga up since and he has not answered the phone."

"I don't know what Bro doing for real, but don't trip. He's gonna show up soon and everything gone be cool. I'll have Quis flame that bitch up though just on GP. Do you know where this shit came from?"

"Manuel. Juan sent them though. He was out the way with my primo making moves, so he said."

"Cool. Well go on about your day, G. I'll find Uno."

I changed my clothes in the warehouse and headed to the shop to collect the rent. We had been letting the barbers work there and just charged them booth rent. Technically, the shop was in my name so I collected the money and handled all of the business.

As soon as I got to the hood, I got pulled over. According to the cop, I did a roll and stop at the stop sign. I knew that it was bullshit because I always made sure I drove carefully. I recognized the cop because he was always in Sunnyside. When he approached the car I was nervous, but I also knew I was clean so I kept my cool.

"License and registration," he demanded.

I unbuckled my seatbelt and grabbed my documents out of my glovebox. He took the information and ran to his vehicle.

When he returned, I asked, "Why am I being stopped, Sir?" That's when he explained to me the alleged offense.

He ranted, "We have to make sure our neighborhood is safe. You could've hit one of the children by not stopping completely."

"I understand. I'll take the ticket." Juan taught me to never argue with the police.

He smiled, "You don't have to get a ticket, Young Lady. Maybe you can tell me what you know about who's dealing drugs in this neighborhood?"

"Sorry, I don't know anything. The ticket will be just fine."

The officer threw my documents in my lap and stormed off. He didn't even give me a ticket. I knew at that moment that they were on to us. Juan was missing and my head started to spin. I wondered if they had him in custody. Luckily, I remembered Kenyon was headed over to the center so I stopped by there after collecting my money.

"K, they on some bullshit mane," I yelled rushing over to him. He silenced me with his hands and directed me into the office.

I grabbed a piece of paper and wrote:
They just pulled me over asking about who selling drugs in the hood. Where the fuck is Juan?

Kenyon responded:
Juan is in custody. They claim they got an anonymous call about him having drugs in his whip. He was clean though so he should be released soon. They took him in for questioning.

"I knew something wasn't right," I stated.

Kenyon grabbed me, " No worries, Sis. Everything is going to be ight. We clean baby. They don't got shit on us and ain't nothing they can do. Stay out the way for a while. Come to the center with the kids everyday. Make your rounds at the salon. You're a legit businesswoman, that's all you need to be focused on. Oh and G…"

"Yeah."

"You're officially out of this shit," he stated walking out of the door.

Sixty-One

When Juan finally got released, he called an emergency meeting for us. Dee ordered take out and we met in their basement.

"These motherfuckers want me bad, y'all. They talking about they received some anonymous calls from the tip line that I'm running drugs through the hood. I don't know who the fuck behind this shit, but believe I'm gone get to the bottom of it."

Kenyon pulled out a folder, "The best thing for us all to do is lay low for now. I got the landscaping business going. G, you got the center and the salon. Of course Dee gone stay working with her nursing. Uno, it's time for you to find something clean to do. They on our asses. We gotta show them we regular, tax paying citizens."

"I agree. When I got pulled over today I was nervous as hell and I knew I was clean. I don't even want to deal with the crooked ass cops at all. Y'all know they don't play fair. Last thing I need is for them to be fuckin with me."

Juan apologized to me. "I'm gone take care of everything, Hermana. I promise they ain't gone be fucking with you. From here on out, y'all can't have nothing to do with the business. All I want y'all to focus on is working and taking care of the kids. Me and K gone handle the street shit."

"It's time to get out," Dee advised.

"We know! We're working on it now. I just need y'all to let us move like we need too. Y'all hold down the kids and the spot."

"Alright. Come on, G. Let's go check on the kids."

Dee and I walked up the stairs leaving Juan and Kenyon behind.

"I know I be on my H-Town shit, K, but I'm ready to separate my bi'ness from Sunnyside. I can't have G or Dee getting caught up in our shit. I got bout six hundred bands worth of work. I gotta get rid of this shit and get the pigs off my ass. I owe the plug two hundred. After that I'm on the move."

"Aye, you remember that nigga Doo Dirty?"

Juan responded, "Yeah I know Doo. I ain't seen him in a minute though."

"He been out the way. His operation in Ohio and shit. Word been serving him some major weight. I know his shit can't fuck with ours. I can make a call."

"You trust dude?" Juan asked.

"I don't trust a soul, nigga! But he in a position to help us get rid of the shit and it takes the heat off of us down here. We still don't even know who this fuckin caller is feel me?"

Juan nodded, "I feel you. Gone head and make the connection. Let's see what this shit about. It can't hurt none."

"I got you," Kenyon confirmed.

"You always do."

Part Seven

Sixty-Two

"So you're just gonna leave?"

"I already told you I was going. I'm not staying in Texas without my family."

Rome snapped, "Am I not your family?"

"You know what I meant, Jerome. You're my boyfriend and I really care about you, but sometimes life goes differently than we plan."

"Griselda, you don't have to leave. You're choosing to go! After all we've been through, I thought I proved that I was in this for real."

Rome and I had grown closer. I decided to stand by his side with the drama with Lillian. Luckily her baby wasn't his. I also got pregnant and had a miscarriage during that time. Rome was right there by my side. Of course I didn't want to leave him, but I knew that my time in Sunnyside was up.

"Why not just come with us? You said that your old position reopened back home. What's so bad about Georgia?"

"I moved here for a fresh start. Home is too comfortable for me. I'm sure you understand that."

"Yes, I feel the same way about Texas. Can you at least promise me that you'll give it some more thought?

Rome agreed and kissed me on my forehead before leaving for work. When he was gone, I called Dee to fill her in on the progress I was making.

"Dee," I screamed when she answered the phone.

"What's up, baby sis? What y'all over there doing?"

"I was packing and arguing with Rome. He is really in his bag about us moving to Georgia."

"Did you expect anything else? I mean the man is up the crack of your ass, girl."

"That's really my boo. It's just weird because this is something Marcus would've understood. He would've told me like 'we're moving with Dee and K, feel me?' Rome don't really understand who we are as a family, which makes it difficult for me."

I heard Dee tell one of the kids to go get Kenyon out of the garage. "Well, G, if he want to be with you then he'll get adjusted. At the end of the day, family is all we have. We've been in Texas our whole lives. It's time to do something different and to show our kids something else."

"You're right."

"He'll come around, trust me. Kenyon just walked in so I'm going to call you back in a minute okay?"

"Who is that?" Kenyon interrupted.

"Get out of my conversation and it's G."

"Tell her I said what up."

"She already hung up. I called you in here because I wanted to talk to you about somethings if you don't mind."

Kenyon sat down, "Talk to me."

"I received an email from the realtor today saying we could pick up our keys and everything went through. What is she talking about, Kenyon?"

"I bought a crib in Stone Mountain."

"Kenyon how did you buy a house without me. I don't even know what the house looks like."

Kenyon grabbed his briefcase and handed Dee the pictures of the home. "It's one of the houses you checked on the list we had. Uno and I went to the A last week to tie up some loose ends and she called about the showing. We checked it out and I loved it. The price was right, so I jumped on it. I couldn't wait to surprise you."

"Surprise me? We agreed that we would rent a condo until we got situated. How you know that Stone Mountain is where we want to live? Did you check out the schools? I work downtown, how far is the commute? These are things we should've discussed first."

"You're being ungrateful, Dee!"

She snapped, "Ungrateful? Are you serious right now?"

"Hell yeah I'm serious. Dee, I've always taken good care of you and our kids. Yeah I fucked up in the past, but I'm a man now. Buying y'all a nice house is something that I'm supposed to do as a father and a husband. You know how many women would be happy to have somebody buy them a house?"

"The house ain't the issue. It's the lack of communication. You and Juan making all these moves and you ain't told me a damn thing."

Kenyon became irate, "I don't have to tell you my every move, Denise. I'm damn near twenty-nine years old. At the end of the day, you're my wife, not my mother. I do what the fuck I please."

"Doing what you please is gonna have you alone and without your family."

He stood up, "If you think you can do better, by all means, do you! I break my fuckin back for you, woman, and I'll be damned if you keep trying to son me. I bought the house, you either move in it or you don't."

Sixty-Three

"My niggas!" Doo-Dirty yelled as Juan and Kenyon pulled in to the parking lot.

They got out of the car and showed Doo Dirty love with a handshake they used to do in Sunnyside.

"What's up?" Juan asked.

"I can't call it. Staying out the way. Getting to this money!"

Kenyon looked around, "Where the hell you got us at, Fam?"

Doo laughed, "Awe we in my little hood. These my folks. We straight out here, ya heard me."

"We in the middle of the woods. Ain't nobody out here," Juan joked.

"My Patna trying to link. We in the same boat, needing a good plug."

Juan and Kenyon got into the car with Doo-Dirty. They had never been to Ohio before, but Youngstown reminded them of Sunnyside. There were a lot of abandoned buildings, trash on the ground and fiends on the corner. Kenyon noticed they didn't see any fast food restaurants or stores on their way.

"Doo you got us in the mud. They getting money roun' hea like we do back home?" Juan inquired.

"A lot of niggas get to it around here. The problem is niggas need good quality work they can get on a consistent basis. That's where y'all come in. I'm just trying to set up the deals and stick my hands in the pot."

Kenyon liked the idea, " You know we gone show love all day. We just really aint trying to be meeting niggas feel me? We can provide you with the work and tickets. Then you distribute that shit according to how you feel. Uno got some samples in the pack. Let niggas test the shit out and see what's good. It's straight cavi so they should be placing orders sooner than later."

"Straight to the point, K. Dot. My folk ain't playing no games. I like that."

Juan laughed, "You know this nigga K.Dot ain't friendly. But you know we move by the code. If they place a large order and we have to bring it, the ticket goes up. If you come and get it, it's even sweeter. We just need to make sure nobody ever knows who we are."

"I dig it. But y'all gotta at least let me show y'all love while y'all in my place. My patna got a spot up the way we can kick it at."

"Naw, we good, Bro. Appreciate it though."

Juan gave Kenyon a funny look, " Fuck what this nigga talking bout. I'm trying to see what the city like, ya dig? Tonight, I'm Rico and I'm bout to turn the fuck up."

"Aight Uno…I see how you rocking. Trust me, I'll never expose my hand. We gone just mix and mingle."

Kenyon was not on the clubbing. He wanted to go to the hotel and chill so they could leave first thing in the morning. "Uno, we chilling tonight. We got way too much to do."

"Drop this nigga off, Doo. We out here tonight. Ol' square ass dude," Juan teased.

After taking Kenyon to Charlie Staples to eat, they dropped him off to the rental car. Juan grabbed his bags and they headed to Doo Dirty's house to get dressed.

"Aye, Uno, get fresh mane. The spot is a hole in the wall, but niggas jump clean feel me? It's gone be a lot of bitches in there, ya hear me? We gone have a good time."

"Already," Juan replied as he opened his suitcase to find an outfit. Although they were on a business trip, Juan was always prepared. He didn't want to be too flashy so he decided to wear an LRG fit. His jeans were discolored and ripped. He had a matching LRG track jacket, T-shirt, and hat. Juan decided to match his outfits with some crispy Air Force One sneakers. They were white with gummed bottoms.

Typically, Juan didn't like to mingle, but he decided to use his looks to connect with a woman in Youngstown. He was looking for someone in the mix who could tell him what was going on. He knew Doo Dirty would lead him right to her.

"Uno, lets roll," Doo Dirty stated after knocking on the door.

Juan opened the door and popped his collar. "You see a real polished Sunnyside nigga in the flesh."

"Sweet Jones!"

"That means it's time to ride out to some Pimp." When they got in the car, Doo Dirty followed Juan's directions and put in UGK. They rapped word for word as the drove to the club.

When they arrived at the bar, Juan was shocked. "Bro, what the fuck is this?" he asked.

"This Jitz. I told you it was a hole in the wall, but this muthafucka be rockin'."

"Fam, my basement bigger than this."

Doo Dirty waved his hand, "Don't let the size fool ya. This the best time you gone have roun' here. Trust me!"

Juan followed behind his friend as he approached the door. Doo-Dirty paid for them to get in and Juan looked around in shock. He saw people smoking, drinking and dancing. The vibe reminded him of Sunnyside and he felt right at home.

"Texas," one man yelled who was holding a camera.

"Aye Rico, this is my nigga BG. He gone get us together with some flicks," he said to Juan.

Juan nodded.

BG responded, "Hell yeah! We gone kick in this bitch tonight."

"Fa sho! My Patna from Texas here so we gotta show him a lot of love."

Extending his hand, BG welcomed "Rico" to the Yo.

"Let us flick up," Juan asked and stood in front of the picture booth. Doo Dirty and a couple of other guys joined them.

After their pictures were finished. Juan ordered a round of drinks. While they waited at the bar, he noticed a girl eyeing him. She was short and thick with pretty brown skin. Juan was especially intrigued by her short hair cut.

"What's yo name?" he asked making his way over to her.

"Key," she stated extending her hand.

"Rico," he responded kissing it.

She grinned, "I ain't never seen you around here before. Where you from?"

"I'm from down bottom. Doo my Patna. I'm just here visiting. You should let me buy you a drink though. What you drinking?"

"Henny."

He laughed, "What you know about yac? I see how you rocking."

Doo Dirty walked up as they were talking. "You good?"

"Of course he good. He here with me," Key snapped.

"Keyshia, chill yo crazy ass out. Don't do it, mane. She's nuts."

Keyshia gave Doo Dirty the middle finger. They were really good friends and joked around a lot.

"He said you were crazy. What kind of stuff you be doing?"

"Don't listen to Texas fat ass. He just salty I spent his brother, that's all. I like a certain type of man and he was not it, but you might be," she flirted.

Juan knew that was her way of confirming she was interested in him. The feeling was mutual and he was ready to see what Ohio had to offer.

Sixty-Four

"It's nice of you to come home and join your family," Dee stated as Kenyon walked into the kitchen.

He didn't respond.

"Oh, you don't hear me, Kenyon?"

"Don't start, Dee. It's too early for this crazy shit."

She threw the pan down, "Nigga you ain't been home in three fucking days! Three! I didn't get the memo that's the kind of marriage we have."

"My bad, Dee. I been out of town with Uno making some moves. Ain't no funny shit going on or nothing like that. I'm just trying to make this little money so we can be comfortable. That's it. That's all."

As they were having the exchange, they heard Amire screaming. They ran up the steps to find her in the middle of the hallway with blood coming out of her mouth.

"K.J., call 911," Dee yelled.

"They gone take too long to come. Go get some towels!" Kenyon instructed as he grabbed Amire and walked her down the stairs towards the garage. Denise grabbed a bag for Amire to use to catch the blood.

Dee drove as fast as she could while Kenyon cradled Amire in the backseat. She had a weak pulse and they were terrified that they were losing her. Luckily, there was a hospital a few blocks up the road. Doctors rushed Amire back for testing immediately. Kenyon and Dee waited in the family room in shambles. Dee knew they needed support so she texted the family to let everybody know what was going on.

After reading the text message, I knew that I needed to go to the hospital. I dropped the kids off to one of the workers at the center and headed to find Juan. When I got to his house, I noticed his cars were there, but he was not answering his phone. Finally, after beating on the door for almost twenty minutes, he answered.

"Why are you beating on my door like you crazy?"

"Bro, Amire is in the hospital. She just started bleeding from her mouth. They don't know what's wrong with her. We gotta get to the hospital."

Juan's eyes got big, "Mierda," he whispered.

When I entered his apartment, I noticed a purse and some sandals in the living room. It caught me off guard because I had never known my brother to allow anyone in his home that wasn't family, especially a female.

"Who do you have in here?" I asked.

"Damn detective. She's just a friend of mines. She visiting from Ohio."

I was confused, "How did you meet somebody from Ohio and what is she doing here?"

"Griselda, I'm a grown ass man. I'm the big brother remember that, chica! Keyshia is cool people. I met her through Doo Dirty and we're getting this money."

"Hermano, we both know niggas can't be trusted. Doo-Dirty shiesty and you know that. I'm not feeling this at all. You need to get this bitch out of here so we can go," I yelled.

"¡Relajarse! Tengo esto," Juan screamed.

"No! I won't chill out cause you trying to make some bitch comfortable. En mamita, I'm not playing Juan."

"Don't be putting nothing on Mamita. I told you everything is cool around here. Trust me, Chica."

Sixty-Five

I heard a few knocks on the door. I rolled over and it was three in the morning. I grabbed my pistol and headed to see who was there. When I looked out the peephole, Rome was standing there in his pajamas.

I opened the door, "What are you doing here?"

"We need to talk," he stated barging in.

"Come in my room; the kids are sleep," I instructed.

I laid back in the bed and Rome sat at the edge where my feet were. "I'm coming with you."

"What?"

"I love you, Griselda. I want to be with you. I just need to know that you're in this. Georgia is a big move. I need to know that I'm a part of your family, your clique or whatever y'all are. I don't want to separate you from your family. My goal is to be a part of what you already have established."

I couldn't believe Rome was actually professing his love and agreeing to move to Georgia with me. Truthfully, I was tired of being alone and wanted to have a family. So Rome was sent from God because I had been praying for that. "Okay," I affirmed his request.

"Promise me that its us til the end, Griselda,"

"I promise."

Rome looked me in my eyes and demanded I get naked. I was so turned on that I slid my shorts off immediately. He went underneath the blanket and started sucking my clit. He used his bottom teeth and top lip to create a rough, yet tender sensation. I could not contain myself.

"Ahhh," I moaned as he continued to please me.

Arching my back I held his head in my hands with my tightest grip. When Rome finally lifted his face, his entire chin was covered in my juices. He wiped his face on his arm and proceeded with sliding his dick into my pussy. His strokes were strong and long. As he glided in and out, I started to flex my pussy muscles.

"Oh shit, baby," he chanted as I moved my body.

As I moved my body, he dug deeper into my insides. When Rome finally flipped me over, I rode his dick with everything I had in me. Marcus used to love when I rode it backwards, so I decided to see if Rome would like that as well. I turned around and started bouncing up and down on his dick while poppin my hips. I couldn't hear anything other than heavy breathing, but I did see his toes curling. Based on that, I knew he was enjoying himself.

"Smack my ass," I instructed as I found my rhythm. Rome pulled my hair and smacked my ass as I did my money dance.

Before he was about to bust his nut, he turned me over and pounded me from the back. I squirmed to the headboard as he penetrated my pussy with all of his might. After we both came, we laid there in our body fluids looking at the ceiling.

Sixty-Six

Kenyon and Juan were getting together to chat about business. "What you got going on?" Kenyon asked.

"This money mission. What else would I have going on?" Juan asked.

"I heard you had a house guest. Why is the broad down here, Uno?"

Juan laughed, "She cool man. That's my bitch."

"You doing way too much. That was only supposed to be about business. Now, you got this chick all in the mix, staying in the crib, cooking that funny ass sausage you eat."

"Its chorizo nigga and that shit smack."

Kenyon snapped, "I'm serious. You really sloppy out here over some pussy."

"It ain't even like that. She came down here to get the pack for Doo Dirty. I fucked her at the crib and G came through. That's when Amire went to the hospital. That was her first and last time at the crib. I didn't think it made a difference since we bout to move anyway feel me?"

"Not really but do you. Just be careful man. We don't know too much about these muthafuckas up the way. That's a whole different territory. Our positions were supposed to be secretive, feel me? You should've had somebody else make the drop. A bitch that knows too much is bad for business."

Juan laughed, "Okay. Papi. Damn! I got you. Dee cook today?"

"I don't know what that crazy ass lady got going on. All we been doing is arguing and I'm tired of that shit. She threaten to leave me every four days out this bitch."

"Dee ain't going nowhere. She just want the best for you. I told yo Keith Sweat crying ass don't settle down at the age of ten. You ain't want to listen though. Remember, you loved her?" Juan joked.

"I do love her. I'm just sick of hearing her bitch all the damn time. My side hoe don't cause me no problems. All she want to do is get fucked and for a nigga to pay a few bills."

"Dee gone kill you and that bitch if she find out. I don't want no parts of that shit. I'm tellin ya now."

Kenyon smirked, "Don't worry about my situation. You need to be worried about Rochelle. What's up with that?"

"Ro is my homie man. She took a bid for me so I'm always gone look out for her. That's Uno's mom so she always gone be my bitch. When she get out, we gone post up in the A and find some shit to do and whatnot. Her attitude just sucks right now cause yo bitch always in her ear."

"She always in everybody's damn ear bout some shit. Aye though, Rochelle sent some pictures to the crib and she thick as fuck. I think she in there dyking though. Ain't no way she getting that thick and her legs aint being spread."

"I hope so. Shit, she can come home and be my little freak. I told you this strip club about to be lit."

Juan handed Kenyon a menu, "Let's go get lunch. You paying though cause I don't have a job. Cutting grass got you smelling like money."

Sixty-Seven

May 15, 2009, our lives changed. Juan and Kenyon hired a team of movers who relocated our things to Georgia. We were official residents of Stone Mountain. It was a bitter-sweet moment. None of us had ever lived anywhere else. We loved Sunnyside, but it was time for a fresh start.

After the movers left with our things, we headed to the neighborhood for a small going away celebration. We didn't want too many people to know we were leaving, therefore we only invited close friends and family. Juan hired Mr. Larry to cater the dinner. We had grilled meat, side dishes and an arrangement of desserts.

Everyone was having a good time and I was so excited to see Alexis walk through the door with Marcus Jr. "Oh my God Lex, I'm so happy you brought him so he could see everybody. You know Mari think he her baby."

"Honey, I didn't have a choice. Bianca has gotten herself into a mess with them pills. Her mother is raising her other baby and asked if I would take Marcus until she got herself together. He's my grandson so you know that wasn't a problem. It's the least I could do for my son."

"We had heard some things about Bianca, but I didn't know it was like that. Girl, I wish that I could take him away with us. Regardless of the situation that's Marcus's blood so he's gonna forever have a place in my heart."

Lex teared up, "I miss my child so much. I think about all of the things I didn't get to say or all of the things we didn't do. I have so many sleepless nights. Having these kids on this Earth is what keeps me going. I'm sad Grandma's girl is moving away, but trust me, I'll be there to visit."

"You better come too, Lex. I want you to stay in Mari's life and I also want to be a part of Marcus's life. Before you leave, I want to give you some money to help with him."

"I can't take your money. You're already raising Mari by yourself. No baby! God will make a way for us."

I wrapped my arms around them, "We're family and I got ya'll. I don't care if ya'll need it or not. I'm gone always do for my people. Marcus wouldn't have had it any other way."

Juan interrupted our conversation. "Come on ya'll; let's pray."

Kenyon said a prayer. We ate good, laughed and enjoyed ourselves. I felt the love in the atmosphere.

I went to look for Juan to share the moment and I found him crying over Mamita's rosary. We both missed her very much and life had not been the same. It was clear that we had lost so much in Texas, but I knew that I still had what I needed the most there and that was love. I was excited for our new journey. Sunnyside definitely sent us off the right way.

Part Eight

Sixty-Eight

We had been in Georgia for a few months and I loved the scenery. What I loved most was there was always something to do. Juan and Kenyon had been back and forth to Texas, so Dee and I spent a lot of time exploring and finding the spots. Oddly, I started feeling ill after a week or so. Rome stated that I had been doing too much and needed to settle down. I wasn't only feeling fatigue, but my body was in pain as well. I made an appointment at the clinic by our house to make sure everything was cool.

Rome had to work so we planned for him to meet me at the clinic. When I arrived he was there waiting, "Where you been?" he asked.

"I stopped by Dee's to check on the kids. She made breakfast for us. I still don't know how you beat me here though."

"I know these Georgia streets," he joked.

"Well hopefully these Georgia doctors can figure out what's going on with me."

Twenty minutes later I was called into the registration room. That was the most embarrassing experience I ever had in front of strangers. I was unaware that I did not have health insurance. Back home, we had a doctor in the hood that we saw. When I gave birth to Mari, Dee handled everything. Having health insurance never crossed my mind.

"No need to worry Ms. We have insurance applications here and you can apply for benefits from the state. Today, we can give you a waiver, which gives you time to get covered before you're billed. Natalie is our nurse, and she's going to take you back to run some tests. Okay?"

"Okay."

I walked behind the nurse who gave me instructions. She made me give them a urine sample. After three attempts she was also able to draw blood. Once all of the testing was done, she sat Rome and I in a room to wait for the doctor.

The Doctor came in with my chart in his hands. He was reading over the results I assumed. "How are we this afternoon," He asked.

"Fine," we stated collectively.

"Great. Well, Ms. Gonzales, I was able to review your test results and we were able to determine why you're feeling down. Your pregnancy test came back positive. All of your other tests were normal. Of course we send the blood samples to the lab and if there's anything of concern there we will call you."

I looked at Rome in utter disbelief. Pregnant? I could not believe it. As distraught as I was, Rome was the exact opposite. His face was lit up like a tree on Christmas Eve. He was so excited that he was going to be a father.

The nurse came back in the room and handed us some pamphlets for OBGYNs and for pre-natal care. I was silent the entire time. Rome was asking questions and gathering information. As crazy as it sounds now, I was not happy about being pregnant. I felt as if I had betrayed Marcus by conceiving a child with another man. I was not certain that I could have the baby and I knew that would cause Rome and I issues. He would not allow for an abortion because of my previous miscarriage.

Sixty-Nine

"Damn, Doo. It's early. It better be an emergency with you blowing my phone up like this, mane," Kenyon stated.

"Have you talked to Uno?" he asked.

"Nah. Last I knew, he was out on his feet. Why? What's wrong?"

Doo Dirty paused, " I need you to come see me. It's important."

"I can't come see you. I got some shit I'm into right now. Can it wait?"

"Nah, it really cant," Doo Dirty stressed.

Kenyon became worried especially because he hadn't spoken to Juan. "Let me check into some things and get back with you ight?"

"Bet."

When the call disconnected, Kenyon called all three of Juan's phones, but they were going straight to voicemail. He called me and asked had I spoke to him and I told him that he was out of town. None of the homies had spoken to him either.

"G, if you hear anything from Uno, have him get with me ASAP," he demanded.

"Okay, K. Is everything okay?" Kenyon did not sound like himself.

"Yeah, just be on alert, okay?"

Something wasn't right and Kenyon knew Doo Dirty was the missing piece. He went to the apartment he had where Tanisha was sleeping. Kenyon and Tanisha had been friends for a few years. One night things escalated and they had been rockin since. When he stormed in he woke her up and had her book Doo Dirty a flight. She booked him a one-way ticket out of Cleveland, Ohio with her pre-paid debit card. Kenyon called and gave him all of the details.

Tanisha noticed Kenyon's vibe was off and became worried, "Bae, is everything okay?"

"Yeah. I'm good, Tee. Business as usual you feel me?"

She nodded, "Just make sure you come back and see me tonight. We've been missing you," she said rubbing her pussy.

"Soon as I'm done handling my business, I got you. I gotta go though. Make sure a car is there to get Doo, okay?"

Kenyon kissed Tanisha and walked out of the apartment. He was on a mission to find Juan.

After driving all over Texas looking for him and making calls to their acquaintances, Kenyon reached a dead end. He finally decided to take a minute to gather his thoughts. There was a Panera Bread on the corner and he pulled in. He went through the drive-thru and ordered a coffee. While he sat in the parking lot, he remembered that there was one place he didn't look. This place was a secret that only he and Juan knew about. They had decided to keep it in case of an emergency. Kenyon went to the warehouse, switched cars and changed his clothes. He wanted to be inconspicuous going to the hideout.

He parked the car at a public place and walked to the location. First he observed the building to make sure the scene was cool. Kenyon remembered the combination to the key code and was able to walk into the space. When he got inside, Juan was laying on the couch watching the news.

"It took you long enough to get here, nigga!"

"Bro, what the fuck? You got a nigga on a wild goose chase looking for your ass! I got G on stand by in Georgia. This nigga Doo-Dirty blowing my shit up at the crack of dawn. The fuck going on, Uno?"

Juan sat up on the couch, "Shit got dirty in Ohio. They set me up, K. The bitch Keyshia calls me and says change of plans. We're meeting at a hotel outside the city. She said the mayor had the city on some zero-tolerance shit and it was hot. I say cool. We had already fucked at the spot she wanted to go to so I was familiar with it. When I get to the joint, she in the room already, naked and shit. So you know me, I start fucking her soon as I seen the pussy. I'm ramming her shit, next thing I know I got two pistols to my head."

"WHAT?"

"Mane, listen…shit got real stupid. These niggas cleaned me out. They took the money, work, and my jewels; everything I had on me for real. Of course they tied me up to a chair and shit. This hoe really set me up for the okey doke."

Kenyon was furious, "Damn, Uno! I told you about that dirty bitch. I knew she wasn't right. Where the hoe at now?"

"I smoked that bitch," Juan replied.

"What the fuck you mean you smoked her?"

"These stupid muthafuckers left the keys to my rental on the table. So I was able to get out of the chair and shit. I cleaned the room down and bounced. I didn't want my prints or nothing left around there feel me? In the whip, I had a strap and some ends. Boom. I bounce and go to her crib. She wasn't there. I swing by Doo's spot and he wasn't there either. I knew eventually she would come home so I broke in her shit. Bout six in the morning she walked in with a duffle bag. Soon as the bitch hit the door I smoked her hoe ass. Tat, tat, tat! I hit her three times. Twice in the chest and one time in the dome. Soon as she was down, I bounced out that bitch."

Kenyon stood there speechless. He was in shock that all of that had transpired.

Juan read his mind, "You know that nigga Doo was in on the shit, right? That's why he calling you. He trying to figure out what happened so he can save his ass. It's over with though for that op."

"I already know! The nigga on his way down here. Let's just play it cool. I want to see what he know and how he riding."

"You know we bout to go to war right?" Juan asked.

"Squad up, nigga!"

Seventy

"Bae, wake up! I need you."

"What, Kenyon?"

"I need you to have G come to the house with the kids and meet me in the hood."

Dee was not feeling Kenyon. He had not been home and she was ready to end their relationship. "No. I can't come to Texas right now. I have a fucking job and kids to raise."

"Look, I know you're salty with me, but right now, I need you. Shit is real and you're the only person in the world I trust right now."

After hanging up on Kenyon, Dee called me and asked me to keep the kids. I asked her what was going on but she didn't know. At that point I assumed the worst. Juan had been missing, Kenyon had been in Texas for the longest and now Dee was headed home. Something was terribly wrong and I prayed to God that my brothers were okay.

Rome came in the room. "Is everything okay, Babe?"

"I hope so. Dee has to go to Texas for a while so we're gonna keep the kids. She shouldn't be gone too long."

"That's cool. I got a few runs to make, but I'll be back. You want me to grab something to eat for everybody?" he asked.

"I have chicken thawing for arroz con pollo for dinner, but you can bring us Chic-Fil-A back," I smiled.

"I got you," Rome smiled before leaving the house.

Dee was clearly in a rush because no sooner than Rome left, she pulled up. She brought the kids bags in the house almost out of breath.

I grabbed the bags from her, "Hey, Sis. What's going on?"

"I don't know, G. I really don't, but trust and believe I'm gone get to the bottom of this shit. Kenyon is about to be wifeless and homeless."

"You gotta chill on K until you know what's going on. He called me a few days ago looking for Juan and I immediately knew something was wrong, Dee. I've been calling Juan for days and have not heard from him. I don't think he's on no bullshit. I think that something went down. Just go make sure that they're okay."

Dee's eyes got heavy. "Griselda, I'm going but I am tired. I don't know how much more of this madness I can take. They stress me out to the max. Every night I toss and turn worried about my husband. At the end of the day, I knew what came with this game, but I thought it would be over by now."

"It will be over soon, Dee. I feel it. Everything is gonna be okay."

Seventy-One

Kenyon had arranged for a car to pick Doo Dirty up and drop him off at the local diner where he was. Knowing that Doo Dirty was involved in Juan's robbery left a bad taste in Kenyon's mouth, but he knew he had to play it cool. When Doo Dirty got out of the car, he walked into the diner looking around. Kenyon waved his hands in the air so that he could see him.

"K. Dot! What's good, mane?"

"What's good, Doo? How was your flight?"

Doo Dirty sat down, "It was straight. I was able to take a little nap before landing. A nigga been stressed the fuck out."

"What's going on, mane?"

"Man, Keyshia got smoked in the city. It's looking all bad because Uno was supposed to be the last nigga that seen her according to her sister. She said that they were linking up."

Kenyon looked surprised, "Hold up. What? If she dead, where the fuck is my brother?"

"Shit that's what I was trying to get with you about. I don't know where he at, mane. They ain't find no dude's body. Keyshia was killed in her crib."

"Come on Doo don't tell me that! I been calling and texting this nigga and ain't heard back from him. Did anybody know that he was the one bringing the dope up there? Maybe somebody tried to rob them or some shit. They be on that ransom shit up the way?" he asked.

"Nah. I ain't heard nothing like that and you know I'm in the streets. Matter of fact this Keyshia's brother, Caddy, calling me now."

Kenyon instructed Doo Dirty to answer the phone. He could tell that he was nervous.

"Yo, Caddy, what's up with it, mane?" he answered.

Caddy on the other end wasn't as pleasant, "You know what's up! We trying to figure out what the fuck happened to Keyshia, nigga. Word is she was with you making a move on that Texas nigga. They find her dead and you niggas ain't nowhere to be found."

"You know it ain't nothing like that. I had a move already set up in the A feel me? Trust and believe I'm trying to figure out what happened my damn self."

"The little niggas told me after the smash, they took the shit to yo spot. There wasn't no problems from what I hear, but how my sister end up dead is what I want to know. Why ya'll ain't kill that nigga, Doo?"

Doo Dirty looked at Kenyon who was looking directly into his eyes across the table. "I don't really want to get into that over the phone, feel me? I'll be back to the city tomorrow. Soon as I touch down, I'm gone holla at you. Shit is crazy though, mane. My patna from Texas missing too, ya dig? I hope ain't nobody get hip and get dirty feel me?"

"For nigga's sake this shit better come out. I don't give a fuck who it is, they gotta die. They killed my muthafuckin sister. I want to know everything you know about this nigga ya heard me. If I find out you had something to do with this shit, I'm at yo head, my nigga. That's on mommas," Caddy yelled before disconnecting the call.

"What he say?"

"They trying to figure out what happened to their sister. Now, the nigga sending threats and shit."

"Against who, Uno?"

Doo Dirty shook his head, "Naw, mane. He threatening me. Talking some shit about I put her on with my people and he was supposedly the last person with her. I ain't got nothing to do with this shit, so I gotta go home and clear this up. My kids there, ya heard?"

"I definitely feel you. I just hope for everybody's sake my brother surfaces. I don't know about that bitch or what she was into. All I know is Juan better be alive or shit gone get ugly. You know the Mexican Mafia don't play no games when they lose one of their own, feel me. Somebody up that muthafucka gone have to answer for this shit."

"I hope Uno okay too, man. When I get back, believe I'm gone try to locate that nigga. I know Key did her business at her people's hotel out the way. I'm gone check the scene and shit to see if anybody saw anything."

Kenyon shook his head, "Bet. Aye, what's the name of the spot they were at?"

"Bel-Air, it's in Hubbard, Ohio," he replied.

"Ight. Keep in touch with me man, especially if you hear anything. Whatever you do, make sure you don't give anybody no information about Uno. When them Mexicans hit the town it's bad business. I don't want your name involved at all. You my people and we gotta stick together."

Doo Dirty left the meeting confident that he had an ally in Kenyon. He did not sense there was anything he should be worried about other than figuring out how to play off the matter to Keyshia's family. Juan being missing put him into a better position. He knew that he needed to come up with a solid story to keep the Mafia and Caddy off of his head.

Seventy-Two

Doo Dirty hopped on a flight and left Texas. Before making it back home, he contacted his girlfriend and advised her to go to Columbus. Her sister lived there and he wanted to make sure his family was out of the city. Caddy was not anybody to play with. Doo Dirty did not want to get caught slipping.

As soon as he arrived in the city, he went to find Caddy. The last thing he wanted to do was avoid them. The truth was he did not have anything to do with Keyshia's murder. He also did not know if Juan was responsible or a victim as well. He wanted nothing more than to disassociate himself from the situation and that's what he planned on doing.

"Caddy," he yelled across the street.

Caddy turned around and saw Doo Dirty's car parked across from their mother's house on Ohio. He quickly ran to the car and got in.

"What's up, Texas?" he asked.

"Mane, I'm trying to wrap my head around this shit that happened. I'm so sorry about Keyshia, mane. You know she was my Patna and like a sister to me."

"I already know. That's why I know you gone help me find out who did this shit. What all do you know?"

Doo Dirty explained, "Key had the little homies ducked in the closet in the room feel me. Dude was supposed to come in with the work and she was supposed to give him the bread. They were supposed to rob them and take the dope and money. The plan was for them to leave Keyshia there tied up and kill Rico. When they got back to the spot, they told me that they couldn't kill dude and Keyshia was with them, feel me? We split the dope and money up and everybody went their separate ways. Me and Peanut bounced to Cleveland to sell the boy and link with some bitches. When I got back to the city the next day, that's when I heard about Keyshia. The fucked up thing is Rico missing too. His people in Texas going crazy because can't nobody find him."

"Word?"

"Yeah man. So I don't know what the fuck happened. Keys told me they left the nigga tied up in the room and bounced. She said she didn't have the heart to kill him because she had love for the nigga."

Caddy leaned back in the seat, "So you don't think that dude had anything to do with Key's getting killed? Ain't it ironic that he missing?"

"He don't know shit about Ohio, Caddy. All he knew is what Keys told him. He didn't even know his way around town. The nigga used a GPS to get to the hotel, feel me? I doubt that he would've been able to find his way to her spot."

Caddy asked, "Besides Peanut and Key, who else knew about the move?"

"I don't know who all these niggas told, but they took Reese little ass with them to clip dude. When they came back, he was with them."

"Dirty Reese?"

Doo confirmed, "Yeah. I told that nigga Peanut he shouldn't have had involved nobody else. He told me Reese was already with Keyshia when he got to the room. I guess she wanted to make sure they had enough muscle."

"Reese and Peanut both were here yesterday paying their respects. Them niggas was moving regular, ya feel me? None of this shit ain't making sense, but trust I'm gone get to the bottom of it. Just make sure you keep yo ear to the streets in Texas. If the Rico nigga surface let me know."

"I'm on it like flies on shit, mane."

When Caddy got out of the car, Doo Dirty was relieved. He felt like speculating that someone else could've been involved took the heat off of him and he knew that gave him time to come up with a plan. He was no longer worried about Kenyon or Caddy. His primary concern was finding Juan or making sure that Juan didn't find him.

Part Nine

Seventy-Three

December 25, 2009, we met as a family in Colorado Springs. Kenyon had booked us a cabin to spend the holidays. I had been experiencing a lot of trouble with my pregnancy, especially with all of the issues Rome and I were having. To make matters worse, Juan hadn't been around much and I desperately missed my parents. The getaway was exactly what I needed at the time.

"Hey, Kenyon…were you able to get a hold of Juan?" I asked.

"I left the message. I'm sure he got it, G."

Dee was making breakfast, "I know he'll be here, G. He's not going to miss the baby's Christmas."

"I hope not. I really just miss the way things used to be. I feel like I'm losing my brother and God knows I can't afford to lose anybody else."

"I know that's right," Dee affirmed.

"Don't y'all worry y'all pretty faces about Juan. Everything is cool, he's just moving accordingly. We're here in these sticks to have fun and enjoy the kids. I'm sure everything is going to work out. Now, I'm bout to hit these slopes with these kids. I hope I don't bust my ass."

Kenyon got the kids dressed and they headed out in the back of the cabin to sled. That gave Dee and I time to talk.

"Have you heard anything from Lex about Marcus?"

"She called me last week and told me that she had full legal custody. Bianca done ended up smoking dope. Lex said she went through the courts so she could get full benefits for him. You know I send them money every month to make sure they are okay. I had talked to Rome about Marcus moving in with us and he had a fit."

"A fit about what? The baby?"

"Girl, he feel like I shouldn't be trying to get a child that's not mine. Especially because I wasn't even trying to have this baby. I just think he's still insecure about Marcus. Honestly, Rome is getting on my last fuckin nerve. I'm ready to call this whole thing off. I don't care that we have a baby on the way. All we've been doing is arguing."

"I already know how you feel. When I finally got my ass to Texas to get Kenyon, I got with him. I had to tell him like he's either in this or he's out. These niggas be so used to us dealing with whatever, they don't realize that we get tired. He's been doing a lot better, but I meant what I said about him being home with his family. Since Juan is getting settled, he dont' have an excuse not to be home. "

I joked, "Girl, I wish Rome would take his ass on for a few days. I'm serious. I need a break. He done texted me five times this morning, trying to act like he was checking on the baby. Now you know he just want to know what I'm doing."

"He's concerned, G. That is his child."

"Concerned my ass."

As we chatted we heard Kenyon and the kids come through the back. They said it was too cold outside and they were ready to eat. I fixed the kids' plates and headed in the living room to sit by the fireplace. I had started journaling and wanted to write in front of the flames.

We were chilling and someone knocked on the door.

"It's Christmas morning. Who could that be?" Dee wondered aloud.

Kenyon opened the door and Juan barged in, "¡Feliz Navidad!" he yelled.

"¡Tio!" Mari screamed before jumping into his arms.

All of the kids proceeded to give him love. I was so happy that I started crying.

"Here she go with the water works," Dee joked.

"Shut up! Y'all know I'm emotional as hell. I missed my brother," I said wiping my face.

"I missed you too, Hermana," Juan laughed as he rubbed my belly.

I wrapped my arms around him and squeezed him as tightly as I could. Juan looked just like Papi. The older he got, the more he resembled our father. Even Dee seemed to notice.

"Uno, you're looking just like Papi."

Kenyon agreed, "You definitely looking like Pops these days. Next you gone be getting grays and shit."

"You ain't too far behind, nigga. While you playing. Anyway, what y'all got to eat around this joint? I'm starving."

"We cooked breakfast. I made huevos and chorizo, it's in the microwave," I replied.

"Just like Mamita used to make. I need parts," he laughed.

I made Juan a plate and we all sat around the table talking and laughing. The morning was perfect. That afternoon, we opened gifts, played games, and ate snacks. Well, that was me doing most of the snack eating. By the time the catered dinner arrived, I was stuffed and could barely keep my eyes open. That night, I fell asleep feeling complete. My whole family was together for the first time in months. My heart desperately needed that.

Seventy-Four

Doo Dirty had received a call that his mother was sick and he needed to come home. Without hesitation, he booked a flight and headed to Texas. When he arrived, his sister was there waiting for him. He got in her car and proceeded to ask her what was wrong with their mother.

"Kim, why you ain't call me sooner? I didn't even know Mommy was sick. We just talked the other day."

"I don't know what's going on. She just all of a sudden said her doctors gave her bad news and she needed us all to get here. I haven't been home in months. You know that."

Doo asked, "How is Alabama?"

"Bama is cool. How is Ohio treating you?"

"Everything is cool-for the most part. Jas is pressuring me into marrying her and moving to North Carolina with her Dad."

"The Carolinas are nice. You'd like it down there. Trust me."

"My first priority is making sure Mama good. If she's not, I'll be moving back here to make sure she gets there."

Kim nodded, "Mama is going to be fine. We just have to get in here and see what's going on. I haven't been in here yet. Soon as I got in I headed right to the airport to get you."

"Oh okay…well let's stop and get Ma some flowers before we go to the house."

Doo-Dirty and his sister stopped at Walgreens and grabbed a card and flowers for their mother. When they arrived at their childhood home, they pulled into the driveway and headed inside.

"Ma," Doo Dirty called out, but didn't hear a response.

Kim walked to the backroom to see if she was back there.

"Sis, is she back there?" Doo Dirty asked.

He didn't hear a response so he walked to the back of the house to see what his sister was doing. When he arrived in the backroom, he not only saw his mother and sister, but Juan was standing there as well.

Their mother was bound to a chair with rope and had duct tape covering her mouth. Kim had been stabbed and was bleeding on the floor.

"What the fuck?" Doo Dirty yelled as he observed the scene.

He looked over to his mother who had tears running from her eyes. Before Doo Dirty could react, Juan made a move. He hit him in the head with his pistol. Doo Dirty stumbled and Juan gagged his mouth with a sock. Then, he tied his arms behind his back. Juan placed Doo Dirty on his knees in front of his mother.

"You know you fucked up, right? How did you think you could set me up and nothing would happen?" Juan laughed.

Doo Dirty tried to explain, but was unable to make a sound.

Juan threw acid in his mother's face and made him watch her skin fall off. She attempted to scream but could not make a sound. Her elderly body could not take the strength of the acid and she slowly started to crash.

Juan laughed as he watched Doo Dirty cry helplessly while his mother burned. He turned to Doo Dirty and gave him a devilish grin before walking out the room. Doo Dirty sighed with relief that Juan didn't kill him as well.

About five minutes later, Juan returned and shot Doo in the back of the head; execution style. His blood splattered all over the walls and carpet, as his head dropped into his mother's lap. Once he made sure they were all dead, he doused the house with gasoline and headed to the garage. He cracked the back door and started the fire. Making sure no one was looking, he hopped the fence and got into the loaner he had parked around the corner.

Seventy-Five

March 9, 2010, I gave birth to my son Jerome JaMar Bryant. He was born at six pounds and eleven ounces. When I had "Mar," Rome and his mother were there. Dee arrived shortly after. Of course Rome and I had to compromise on his name. Thankfully, his mother and Dee were there and helped us come to an agreement.

My son was so handsome and reminded me of Mari when she was born. He also favored Baby Juan. I couldn't wait for them to see her. Kenyon was at the house with the kids and said he would bring them to the hospital later on to see us.

Dee's phone rang and she told me that she had to go and would be back later on. She seemed to be in a hurry so I assumed Kenyon needed her to come help with the kids. At least I wasn't alone though. Both Rome and his mother were there.

"How are you feeling, Griselda?" she asked.

"My back is hurting a little, but other than that, I'm fine."

Rome handed me another pillow to put behind me, "They said they were gonna bring the baby back once they finished his circumcision."

"Get you some rest, Baby, while he's gone. We'll wake you up when they bring him back."

I was still doped up and extremely tired. I dozed off feeling comfortable that Rome and his mother would make sure the baby was okay.

Rome's mother handed him a paper once I was finally sleep. "This is the information for the safe deposit box. Your grandmother's rings are in there."

"Ma, I don't think we're ready for marriage. We're still young and have some things to work out in our relationship first."

"You should've thought about all of that before you got her pregnant. Your father and I stressed the importance of family to you all of your life, Jerome. There's no way you can make a child and not make an honest woman out of the mother. You know that."

Jerome knew that his parents wanted him to marry me and he tried to avoid it as much as possible. "I'll think about it, Ma," he said to get her off of his back.

"The only thing you should be thinking about is when you're going to propose, Jerome. This is not an option."

"Ma, why are you trying to force me into marriage. You know that I'm going to be a father to my child. I would never abandon him. I have nothing to lose by choosing to wait for marriage. Don't you want me to make sure Griselda is the one for me?"

His mother grabbed her purse, "I'm going to get a soda. And son I raised you. I know that you're going to be an amazing father. Just remember that I am in charge of your inheritance. Now don't shame our family. I trust that you're going to do the right thing."

Rome's mother left the room and he dropped his head in his hands. His grandfather left him an inheritance and he refused to let anything stand in the way of him receiving his money. He knew that his mother was vindictive enough to keep him from getting it, so he knew that he would have to marry me.

Despite loving me Rome was still unsure about our relationship because of my connection to Marcus. Prior to me giving birth, we were fighting a lot about Marcus Jr. For the sake of our relationship I decided not to get him until Rome was more open to it. He agreed to revisit the conversation once things were settled with the baby. Although my heart was set on raising Marcus Jr., I knew Rome was right. My focus needed to be on my son, Mari and The Squad.

Seventy-Six

When Denise arrived on her street, she was stunned to see her house surrounded by policemen. She stopped at the end of her driveway and jumped out of the car.

"What is going on here?" she yelled.

One of the detectives informed the other that she was the woman in the picture. The office instructed Dee that she needed to go inside of the house. She walked through her garage, escorted by the officer and could not believe her eyes. Her house had been ransacked.

"Ma'am, we would like to ask you a few questions about your husband and Juan Gonzales."

Dee spazzed, "Where are my kids?"

"Your kids are safe and depending what you give us, they'll be back with you as soon as this is over."

"I don't have anything to say to you. Am I under arrest?" she snapped.

"No ma'am you are not under arrest. We'd just like to obtain any information you may have about Mr. Gonzales's whereabouts."

Picking up her phone, she texted her lawyer. Dee could not believe that their home had been raided. She assumed that Kenyon was in custody and she needed to get to the kids. The detective handed her the search warrant. She grabbed her keys and hopped in her truck.

"Shit!" she yelled. Dee knew that she was clean, but had no clue what Kenyon and Juan had been into.

She was finally able to connect with the lawyer who was meeting her downtown where both Kenyon and the kids were.

When Dee arrived, the lawyer was there waiting, "Mrs. Green, how are you?" he asked.

"I am losing my mind. Please tell me what the hell is going on? They tore my house up!"

"From what I gathered, they are looking for Mr. Gonzales. According to the detective, he is the person of interest in an organized drug ring. They received a call on the tip line stating that your husband was storing the drugs. That is how they were able to obtain the search warrant. Luckily, your home was clean and they have no reason to keep Kenyon."

Dee threw her hands in the air, "Thank God!"

"They are going to be watching you guys. Make sure that you guys have no interactions with Juan. He is wanted and you can be charged for harboring a fugitive. The kids are in a room with a social worker. We can go and get them now."

Jane Kline, the lawyer, escorted Dee to the social worker that the kids were with. She signed them out and waited to see if Kenyon would be released as well. The lawyer advised her to take the children home and she would bring Kenyon once he was released.

Dee couldn't contain herself. When she got all of the kids strapped in the car she broke down. Life as we knew it was officially over. The police had made their way to us and she knew that it was only the beginning of trouble.

"Everything is going to be okay, Mama" KJ said attempting to comfort his mother.

Amire and Mari were in their feelings as well. They joined Dee in crying. The raid had scared the life out of them and they had no clue what was going on. No matter what we did in the streets, we always kept it away from the kids. Apparently, we were not careful enough.

Seventy-Seven

"Ms. Gonzales, these detectives are here to talk to you," the nurse advised as she woke me up from my nap.

"For what?" I asked.

The detective opened his notepad, "Ma'am we are looking for your brother; Juan. Do you know where he is?"

Rome stood up, "Do y'all have to do this now? She just had a baby, for Christ's sake."

"We understand this is uncomfortable, but we're looking for your brother. Do you have any idea where he could be?" the other detective asked.

I snapped, "I have not spoken to my brother, okay? I've been too busy trying to deliver my child. I don't know where he is or what he has going on. I can't help y'all so please leave."

The detective became belligerent. "Harboring a fugitive is a felony offense. If you know where he is, you will be charged as an accomplice."

"I just told you I don't know where he is so get the fuck out! If you need to talk to me about anything else, please find my lawyer."

The nicer detective gave Rome his card as they exited the room. Soon as they were gone, I broke down. I couldn't believe they came to the hospital looking for Juan. I didn't know where he was or who he killed for that matter. As I was sobbing, the hospital phone rang.

"Hello," Rome answered it. "Okay, thanks, Dee."

"What Dee say?" I asked.

"She told me to go check out the crib. They raided their spot looking for your brother and could've gotten yo crib too."

I lost it, "Oh my God!" I screamed.

"Calm down, Griselda. The last thing you need to do is raise your blood pressure. I'll go to your house and make sure everything is cool. If you don't want to go back to your house, y'all can come stay with me."

I nodded.

Rome grabbed his keys and headed to my house. I was so hurt. My brother was my everything. I did not want anything to happen to him. I prayed, "Mary, please protect my hermano. Mamita, if you can hear me please look out for Juan. I need you to send your angels now more than ever. Forgive our sins. Amen."

Seventy-Eight

Juan had been indicted by a grand jury for drug trafficking. They were able to charge him because of a snitch. Apparently, they had been watching the shop in Texas. One of the little homies, Melo, got caught with drugs and a gun. In exchange for immunity, he had a to wear a wire on Juan.

When he got word that we all had been raided, he decided to turn himself in. They had detectives parked outside of our homes. They even froze Kenyon and Dee's assets since they believed Kenyon was connected. I could not believe how quickly things turned for us. Regardless of what they were saying, I was going to ride for my brother. Everybody else laid low but Rome and I showed up for Juan's arraignment.

"You okay?" he asked as we sat in the courtroom waiting to see Juan.

"I'm okay," I replied.

After almost two hours, it was finally Juan's turn to see the judge.

The prosecutor stated, "Your honor this is case #218790, the state of Texas versus Juan Carlos Gonzales."

"Mr. Gonzales, you are being charged with first degree drug trafficking and conspiracy to transport an illegal substance across state lines. How do you plead?"

"Not guilty," Juan stated.

"Your honor, we are requesting that the defendant be remanded until trial. He has ties with a drug cartel and is very dangerous."

Juan's lawyer objected, "Your honor, these charges are ridiculous. A prosecutor thirsty for convictions is framing Mr. Gonzales. He has no prior arrests and there has been no confirmed affiliation with any drug organization. These charges are frivolous and without merit."

"Save the specifics for trial. The charges against Mr. Gonzales are serious, and therefore this court must do its diligence to society. Mr. Gonzales will be held on a one million dollar bond, cash or surety. Pre-Trial is scheduled for July 19, 2010. Court is adjourned," the judge stated before slamming the gavel.

Juan seemed unbothered. I think it was because we were financially able to get Juan out. I was ready to put up the salon and anything else I had to in order to get my brother home.

"Good news! You guys can visit with Juan this afternoon. He is being returned to the county jail and I've scheduled you for 4pm. Is that okay?"

"That's fine. Our flight does not leave until tomorrow." I replied.

"Awesome. Well, I have to be in another hearing in about twenty minutes. I'll be in touch. You folks have a good day."

The lawyer left Rome and I standing in the middle of the courthouse.

"Everything is going to be okay, G. Your brother is far from a fool."

"What do you mean by that?"

Rome stated, "Juan just does not seem like a guy that will go away without a strong fight. I could tell by his expression that he's working on a way to beat this."

"I hope so, Rome, because I cannot take anymore losses."

"My Mom always says the Lord works in mysterious ways. You never know what he has planned. All you have to do is trust in his will. Okay?"

I nodded in agreement.

Rome and I had lunch at a restaurant close to the courthouse before our visit. We talked about the kids, purchasing a new home and me possibly opening a beauty shop in Georgia.

Finally, it was time for us to go back to the jail. Juan was housed on the fifth floor. When we got off of the elevator, he was behind a glass wall. They had cream, plastic chairs set up in front of each window. Rome pulled the chair out for me and stood behind me.

"¿Como estas?" I asked picking up the phone.

"I'm great," he laughed.

"Are you sure, Hermano?"

"Yes, G. Please don't worry about me. I am fine! You have to trust that your brother is a guerrero."

I wasn't trying to hear what he was talking about. "Whatever! We're going to get you out of here. You can come home until this trial is over."

"Give Rome the phone." I was surprised, but I handed Rome the receiver.

"Look man- I know we don't really know each other, but I need you. While I deal with this mayhem, I need you to make sure my sister and the babies straight. I need you to stand in and do what I can't do."

Rome smiled, "No problem, Brother. I love Griselda and the kids. Anything I can do for them, I definitely will."

"I appreciate it. It felt good seeing you by her side in court today."

"She's my lady. I wouldn't have let her come all the way to Texas alone. Once I knew that the kids were safe, not coming wasn't an option."

Juan smiled, "I like the way you move, Rome. Real recognize real."

"Well, you take care of yourself in here and let me know if there's anything I can do for you while you're in here."

"Actually, I need ya'll to put some money on my books. They think I'm some kind of kingpin and I had twenty-eight dollars on me when I turned myself in. Anything you can spare would be helpful."

"What does he need?" I asked after hearing Rome say, "I got you."

"Here," he handed me the phone.

"Bonita, Rome is going to put a few dollars on my account. Make sure you also put money on your phone so I can call and talk to the kids."

I responded, "Already. You know that I'll do anything I can for you without a doubt. They said downstairs that you needed white under clothes. When the visit is over, I'll go grab some things from WalMart."

"That's cool. Make sure you get a large. I can't be in here in no young shit. A nigga might try me thinking I'm sweet or something."

"Naw, I'm sure they already know what it's hitting for."

As we were laughing the guard approached Juan, "Visit Over," he yelled.

"That's my Hermana. Aye, make sure you tell Bro I love him. BAU."

"Already," I responded and then I watched them take my brother away shackled in chains.

Part Ten

Seventy-Nine

Juan had been away for almost a year waiting on his trial to start. There had been a lot of issues with the state's case, in which the judge continued to grant them continuances. Juan demanded that we continue on with our lives so that's what we tried to do.

Rome and I had moved into a new home, things were going well for us. He had accepted a promotion at his job and I enrolled in nursing school. Dee had hooked me up with a program that her job offered. I wasn't going to be a Registered Nurse, but I was content with my LVN degree for the time being.

School and work kept me extremely busy, but I was so excited for everyone to be at our home celebrating Mar's first birthday. We decided to have an Elmo theme since that was his favorite character. Rome's mother and Dee got all of the decorations and laid our backyard out.

"Hey, Babe, is there anything else you need me to do before I leave?" Rome asked.

"Can you just make sure that you get the cake on time?"

He showed me his phone, "I already have it saved on my calendar, Babe. My phone is going to alert me an hour before."

"Cool. I'm about to go to Sam's Club and get the ice and ice cream cups. Ma and Dee got everything else we needed. Dee said they made the candy bags last night."

"I love Dee! She's always coming through in the clutch. We're gonna have to do something nice for her soon. I appreciate her keeping the kids when I get called in to work."

"Yes, your hours have been crazy lately. I'll be glad when they go back to normal."

"Me too, love. Me too."

Mari busted through the door. " Umi, can I go outside and play?"

"Not right now, Pooh. We have to get ready to go to the store and get the rest of the stuff for Mar's party. When we come home you can, okay?"

"Okay."

After kissing Rome, I grabbed the kids and headed out the door. It took me an hour and a half to get everything I needed. When I arrived at home, Dee and Ma were there setting up.

"Hola, Ladies," I yelled.

"Hey," they replied.

"It looks so good out here. Thank y'all so much."

"You know I would do anything for Grandma's little monster. It has been my pleasure," Rome's mother stated.

Dee hugged me, "Girl, nothing has changed. I will always have your back."

" I appreciate yall. Oh dang, its almost two thirty. Have y'all heard anything from the party company? I think the characters are supposed to be here in an hour or so."

My phone rang just as I was about to check my email for the confirmation.

"This is a collect call from Juan. This call is from a correctional facility and may be monitored and recorded."

I accepted the call, "Perfect timing! Everybody is here. We're getting ready for the party. You should see your son running around my backyard."

"Man, I can only imagine how he moving. You know I had quick feet as a jit as well. I'm so salty I'm not there with y'all, G."

"You know I wish you were here as well. I've been calling your lawyer every other day. He said that they just keep postponing. I don't know how they keep allowing them more time. They either got a fuckin case or they don't."

"He said they were supposed to be releasing some new information in a few days from some damn witness. They got homie in witness protection and shit. I don't know what they on, but I have a right to face my accuser so they better get them in the courtroom. I'll be damned if I go out like this."

I went and grabbed Mari and Baby Juan so he could talk to them. "Just keep your head up and stay focused. It's going to all turn around. Here are the kids."

"Tio!" Mari yelled.

"Hi, Tio's baby, I miss you so much. How are you?"

Mari smiled, "Good! I miss you too. You want to talk to Juan?"

"Yeah put him on the phone. Love you."

Juan grabbed the phone from Mari, "Lo!"

"What's up son? Damn. Daddy love and miss you so much."

"Miss you too. Bye," Baby Juan replied before handing me the phone.

"Damn!"

I laughed, "You know he on the run. Can't keep them still for a minute. Plus, all of these people just arrived so they are turnt."

"I'm glad they're having a good time. I ain't gone hold you too long. You know I love y'all. Make sure you take pictures and put them in the mail."

"I will. Love you, Juan."

"Love you too, hermana," he said before the call dropped.

Eighty

"Well- it's about damn time you answered this muthafucka," Juan complained.

"My bad, bro. I been hella busy with work and school. What's good with you," Kenyon asked.

"I'm doing alright. Just ready to know what the fuck is going on for real. These muthafuckin prosecutors on some bullshit, K."

Kenyon went into his home office and shut the door, "Remember that paperwork that fell in my lap? I was going through that shit again trying to connect the dots. I found something I'm gone have yo people take a look into. I don't want to go into too much detail yet, but it could be gold."

"My nigga! I knew I could count on you. I'll have the Jews contact you and check it out. What's up with the fam though?"

"Everybody good. I almost had to put the screws to KJ's little ass the other day. He really feeling himself. I keep telling him he don't know shit about the streets, he was raised in the burbs. Dee, running around here cussin us all out as usual. Amire doing a lot better and Baby Uno a fuckin savage."

Juan laughed, "That's my seed! Did you expect anything less from him. You heard from his Mama? The stankin hoe ain't wrote me back yet."

"Actually, Dee mentioned some shit about her coming home in six months. She did some kind of program and they're letting her come home I guess."

"Word? Yeah alright. I'd like to know more about that program my damn self."

Kenyon sensed Juan's concern, "You know I'll pull the demo and let you know what's up."

"Most definitely. Anyway, have you talked to Gris?"

"We had dinner with them the other night. You know old boy popped the question and shit. Rome is cool and all, but it's something about him I can't really fuck with."

"She wrote me on JPay and told me she was getting married. I wasn't too thrilled but she seems happy so I don't got no choice but to roll with the punches."

"Yeah, I guess so huh," Kenyon added.

"Just make sure you keep an eye on that muthafucka. I don't want him to think shit sweet because I'm out the way right now."

"He don't seem like that kind of cat. I just think he sneaky. G on her toes so there's no doubt in my mind she gone be straight."

"That's that Sunnyside shit."

"You already know."

The operator interrupted, "There is one minute remaining on this call."

"Welp, that's my hint. I love you. Send a nigga some pictures of the kids."

"I got you," Kenyon stated before hanging up the phone.

Eighty-One

"I thought I would love having a big house, but it is so much to clean. I'm thinking about hiring a service," I complained.

"Girl, I make Kenyon and the kids clean our house. I'll be damned if I work, cook and clean all day long. Then the nigga got the nerve to want me to suck dick and throw it back."

We laughed.

"Dee, something is truly wrong with you. At least K be on it. I gotta damn near rape Rome these days. I don't know what's going on with him. Shoot, I thought our sex life would be crazy since we're newly engaged."

Dee shrugged, "Yeah he's trippin. Now is the perfect time to go dumb."

"Apparently his job is really stressful. I kind of wish he didn't take that promotion because his hours are crazy. I barely see him and the kids are being raised by his mom. She don't mind but I be wanting them to be at home."

"Once you're done with your program you'll have more time to be with the kids. This is just the sacrifice you have to make right now. It'll all be worth it though."

I closed my bedroom door to make sure Rome couldn't hear what I was about to say next, "I wanted to ask you something. If I marry Rome, would he be entitled to all the money I have?"

"What do you mean?"

"You know we have the insurance money from Marcus and then I have the bread I stashed. You've been investing all of our ends, plus we got the restaurant. I'm not trying to give any of that up, especially with Juan being gone."

"Y'all can sign some type of premarital agreement basically stating that you both retain any assets or debt acquired before the marriage. Then whatever y'all obtain while married can be split down the middle if necessary."

I nodded, "Okay cool. I don't think he would mind that. Especially since he would inherit all of his parents' assets and stuff."

"Do you know anything about his finances or assets?" Dee asked.

"Honestly, we never talk about money. I've still never been to his job. All I know is he does make more money now then when we got together because he pays the mortgage. His credit is good because we didn't have any issues securing the loan for this house. It's in his name and we planned on adding mines once we got married. I didn't want to overdo it since I still own the condo so I didn't sign."

"That was smart, G. Just before it gets too close to the wedding make sure you guys discuss y'all finances. You definitely need to know more before y'all get hitched. Rome probably got a bomb ass retirement and some investments."

"He's definitely good with his money and his people got some paper. I know it ain't all come from the church either. I told you his parents just got that house built on the lake. That mug is so nice! They definitely blew a bag."

Dee clapped, "That's exactly why you need to know what that nigga got. Shit, if nothing else Mar is entitled to a piece of that pie. Just make sure you don't mention anything about what we have as a family. Our stuff been solid because nobody knows. I know ya'll getting married, but some stuff gotta stay between family."

I agreed, "That's why I asked you just to make sure I wasn't going too far with it."

"G, go be happy with that man. Just be careful that's all. You deserve the love and commitment Rome is offering you."

"Hey, son, are ya hungry?"

"Yes ma'am. Can you make me some sausage links? I've been working all night."

Rome's mother poured him some coffee.

"So what's going on? How is Griselda and my grandboy? I haven't seen them in a few days."

"Everything is going well. She's just trying to decorate the house and get the kid's rooms together. I was thinking about taking them to Florida for a family vacation. The kids have never been to Disney."

"That'll be nice, baby. Maybe Pops and I can join you all. Have ya'll made any plans about the wedding?"

Rome sighed, " Honestly, I want to hold it off at least a year or two. I just want to make sure she's completely healed from the death of Mari's father."

"Just give her time, Rome. The trauma she's been through takes time to break down and heal. I think she's doing a good job. She's opened her heart to you, she's given you a child, and now she's making a home for you all. That itself speaks volumes."

"I know, Ma. I love her, I really do. My goal is just to make sure everything is good before we exchange vows. I don't want to go before God and our hearts are not completely synced. You have nothing to worry about though. I promise I'm gone do the right thing, Mama."

Rome's mother smiled and handed him a plate of bacon and eggs. The remainder of the afternoon, they sat at the table talking and drinking coffee.

Eighty-Two

"Good afternoon, Juan. How are you?"

Juan sat up in his chair, "Talk to me, Fred? I'm ready to get this show on the road."

"Well, I'm going to be straight with you, Juan. They prosecutors are willing to negotiate."

"What do they want from me? I know how this shit works," Juan replied.

Fred, one of Juan lawyers, handed him a document. "They are willing to give you immunity and protection in exchange for your connect."

Juan gave Fred a stiff look, "Oh yeah? If this is what they're offering me, then these crackers ain't done their research. I'm not giving them shit. I don't know shit."

"I'll be honest with you. This is our only option, Juan. We reviewed the wire tapes and they don't have much there. You hear two voices making the drug deal, but your name, specifically, is never said. They've referenced you as Uno, but there's no mention of Uno or Juan on the tape. Their witness actually greets the other voice as OG. The problem for you is they have the direct witness. He is going to testify at trial that you were in the car with him."

Juan responded, "You sound worried, Fred. I've paid good money for you to get me out of this mess. One witness ain't nothing. They found a bottom feeder who thirsty for a deal because he's too pussy to take his time like a man. I ain't bowing down to that hoe nigga or these fucked up prosecutors."

"Our firm will do everything in our power to beat this case, Juan. You have my word. They still have discovery information that has not been released. As we get closer to trial, they will start to unveil their entire case. In the meantime we will continue to investigate and build the strongest case we possibly can. Do you have anything that we can potentially use to discredit this witness?"

"Nah. I don't even really know this clown. I've seen him around, but I'll see what I can find out. One of my comrades may know more. He said that he had some information that could potentially help me with my case. I'm assuming it may be information about this Carmello kid."

Fred stood up, "Juan, listen to me okay? Make sure that whatever information you get is done so under appropriate circumstances. I don't want to run the risk of the prosecution trying to claim the witness was sought out or the information was illegally obtained."

"No worries, Fred. Trust and believe I'm focused on coming home. Ain't nothing gone get in the way of that. I don't need any more problems with these muthafuckas."

After shaking hands, Fred gave Juan his blessing and ended the meeting. Juan knew that the prosecution was busy and he wanted to make sure he was ahead of them when it came to his case.

As soon as he was put back on his block, he grabbed the phone and called me.

"Hola, Hermana," he stated.

"¿Hermano, que pasa?"

"Everything is good. My lawyer just left here. We were going over the case. Based on the evidence that has been presented, I decided that I'm going to trial. There's no way I'm gonna let these muthafuckas do this bullshit to me."

I was concerned, "Are you sure that you want to do this? I mean the lawyer said you were looking at almost twenty years if you were found guilty."

"Griselda, I'm a man. I stand on principles. Like I've always told you, don't ever compromise your principles out of fear. There's warrior in our blood. They're accusing me of something that by nature, I'm not guilty of. I would be a coward to cop out to this bullshit."

"Juan, I don't think that's being a coward. I think it's just playing the game. You have the kids to think about. There's no way you can raise them behind bars for twenty years. Not only do they need you, but I need you too."

Juan was silent for a few seconds, "And no matter what, you'll always have me. Just make sure that you always be my voice, G. Never let them silence us. Our family stood for something. We changed the way niggas moved in our hood. Grandma's lights stayed on because of the love and loyalty we showed Sunnyside. If my life ain't worth nothing else, it's worth the legacy I created."

"You know that I will always have your back. Nothing can ever come between us. I promise you that I'll always be there no matter how this plays out. I'm against this trial shit, but I will support whatever decision you make because you're making it as a man."

"Already," he replied.

"Uno was asking about you yesterday. His bad ass then punched Mari in the face. Had my baby on swole. I almost jacked him up."

"What? Awww nah he can't be hitting on my baby. You should've lumped his little ass up, G. He gotta know he can't be hitting on women. Is he still over there?"

I had to give Juan some news about his family that I wasn't sure he was ready for. "Well, he's gone. I don't know if you've heard or not, but Rochelle is getting out in a few weeks. Something about a program she completed and good behavior. She's decided to, of course, come get Uno and she told me that she plans on moving with her brother Junior, who's stationed in Florida."

He snapped, "That bitch ain't taking my son to no fuckin Florida. See, I knew Rochelle was gone get out and be on some bullshit. I set everything up for her to come home and be straight. Georgia is the best place for them. How the fuck she gone take him away from the only family he's known? Her bitch ass brother ain't about shit."

"Calm down."

"Man fuck all of that. When you see that bum ass bitch, tell her I'm looking for her. It don't make sense that she's getting out so soon anyway. G, don't trust Rochelle. She's bitter and she trying to be spiteful with my son and I ain't on that shit. If she take him to Florida, I'll never see him again. Hell nah. You gone have to tell her she can't take him."

"Hermano, I can't tell her what to do with her son. I can only suggest that she stays here, but it's her life. Ro has been through a lot and she's entitled to a fresh start."

I know Juan was upset, "G, I love you, but I'm not feeling how you rockin. Tell K I'm gone be hitting him from the hot spot this evening. Ight?"

"I'll tell him when we hang up. I love you too, Juan. Just consider what I'm saying. All kids want their mothers. Imagine what our lives would've been like if we didn't have Mamita."

He didn't respond. Instead, he hung up the phone without saying goodbye. I did not want to tell Juan about Rochelle, but I knew that I had too. Had he heard it from someone else, he would have questioned my loyalty. I wanted to make sure that no matter what, he knew that I wasn't folding.

Eighty-Three

Kenyon answered, " Bout time you called. I been sitting here waiting for a cool little minute."

"You know I had to make sure shit was sweet before I hopped on this burner."

"I already know. What's good though?"

Juan explained, "The lawyer came down here today. He gave me the rundown. They case weak besides this Melo clown. Dude supposed to come give them a direct account of what they couldn't get from the tapes and shit."

"They tried to offer you some bullshit deal huh?"

"Hell yeah. He like they said I can go home a free man with protection if I give them a connect. They want the plug and access to the big load of work."

Kenyon smirked, "Them some dirty muthafuckas, Bro. They only want access to the shit for their own personal gain. I'm already hipped to these pigs. I been on my inspector gadget shit and I got something that's gone change this whole shit up."

"Oh yeah," Juan asked.

"Let's just say they gotta do a better job of hiding. I went through all the shit I had and put some shit together. There's a pattern to how they do the shit and I figured it out. So relax my guy, you'll be home."

"That's what I like to hear my nigga. Straight to it -no games. Just be careful. You know they on us like flies on shit."

Kenyon agreed, "You ain't never lied, but trust and believe I'm on my shit. They can't do nothing but congratulate me on being on the dean's list."

"Haha, you a cold muthafucka, K."

"Let you tell it. I gotta break out though. Get back with me in a few days."

"Fa sho. Aye, G, told me some shit about Ro coming home. What you know about that? She said this bitch trying to take my son to Florida."

He sighed, "Man, I don't know what the fuck is going on with Rochelle. On some real shit, I've been trying to stay out of it all. I'm still trying to figure out how she finessed her way home. You know I checked into it and I didn't see no black and white. I told Dee that she wasn't taking Uno to no fuckin Florida though. Of course we had it out about that shit too. That's why I been easy on the situation."

"Just make sure you advocate on my behalf when it's time. Griselda a woman so she supporting this bullshit like ain't nothing wrong. She told me that's his Mom and he want to be with her. I was thinking he don't even know that hoe."

"Uno be doing video visits and going to see her so he know who she is. He so attached to G and Dee it's gone be hard for Rochelle to break that. Right now we can't worry about that though. We gotta worry about getting you home and then we can deal with whatever else."

"You're right. I love you, Nigga," Juan expressed.

"Love you too," Kenyon responded before disconnecting the call.

Eighty-Four

Dee was downstairs cooking breakfast when Kenyon walked down the steps.

"Hey, what are you making?"

"I told the kids I would make waffles and sausage this morning since I've been so busy this week. I cut up some fresh fruit if you want some."

Kenyon poured himself a glass of orange juice and sat at the table watching Dee.

"I love you," he stated.

"I love you too, negro. What's wrong?"

"Why something gotta be wrong? I'm just showing my woman some love that's all."

Dee smiled, "Thank you, husband. I really appreciate it."

"I was thinking that we could take a vacation next month. Just you and I. We need a break from everything ya know? Some time for us to just get back to the love and enjoying each other's company."

"I would really like that, Kenyon. I'm not gone lie- ya girl is tired. With everything that has happened in the last year, I'm just drained. I talked to Auntie Jane this morning and she was telling me that Mommy ain't been feeling too good. Now, I feel like I made a mistake leaving Texas without her."

"You know we could always move her here with us. We got all of this space, not to mention Rochelle's house that Uno got her is here as well. I just don't know if Ma ready to leave Texas. She's been there all of her life."

Dee cut her eyes at Kenyon, "Now, you know it's gone be hell convincing that woman to leave her house. Jane cannot take care of her. Junior is in the military and they move around too much for her to be with them. That's why I don't know how he talked Rochelle into coming down there. I can't worry about all of that though. My focus is on our family and making sure my mother is okay."

"We on the same page with it, Bae. You remember I told you that I had to leave for the day? I should be back sometime this evening. I'll make sure I check in though, so you're not worried."

"No more blood, Kenyon. I don't know what you got going on and I truly don't want to know. You know them people watching us, so don't do anything stupid."

Kenyon stood up and grabbed Dee's waist. "Now you know I ain't about to do nothing to jeopardize what we got going on. You got my word. All I'm doing is peepin the scene out to see what's what."

"As long as that's all it is, Kenyon Green."

"Chill out with my government, woman," he joked.

Dee wrapped her arms around Kenyon's neck and kissed him on the lips. He slapped her on the butt before heading upstairs to get ready.

Eighty-Five

Kenyon loaded his landscaping equipment in the back of the pick up truck he had. His drive was almost an hour and a half to Phoenix City, Alabama. It was a small town across the border from Columbus, Georgia. When he arrived in the city, he immediately went to the abandoned property he had found. For the last couple of weeks, Kenyon had been back and forth to the area doing his research.

Once he felt safe, he went into the home's basement and changed. For this mission he was able to find a dreadlock wig and an artificial mustache. He also purchased reading glasses to professionalize his look. After dressing, Kenyon headed back out to the truck and proceeded to his target location.

The diner where he was going sold Soul Food brunch. It was one of the hottest spots in the small town. He drove around the building to check for cameras. There was one in the back where the deliveries were made so he decided to enter from the front entrance. As soon as he entered, the young hostess sat him in the back of the diner, per his request. Kenyon ordered a coffee and requested the local newspaper.

"Sir, are you ready to order?" the waitress asked after about five minutes.

"What is the chef's special?" he asked.

"This afternoon we're serving our famous stew. It has greens, peppers, cabbage, corn, chicken, rice and hot links. Most folks enjoy it with our peach tea and fried chicken."

"That sounds amazing! I reckon that's what I'll have."

"Good choice," she replied before taking Kenyon's menu.

While waiting for his food, he observed the diner. There were a lot of elderly couples enjoying their meals. Children were having ice cream and the aura was very friendly. When his food arrived, he was starving. Kenyon hadn't removed his gloves, but he decided to do so when he started eating his chicken. As he indulged, he looked up briefly and that's when he spotted Carmelo. He was dressed in a white t-shirt, black slacks and apron. It appeared that he was one of the line cooks.

The waitress interrupted Kenyon's observation, "Sir, can I welcome you to our sweet potato pie?"

"I'd love that, Honey. Could you pack it up to go?" he asked.

She agreed before heading behind the counter. While waiting on his pie, Kenyon overheard Carmello letting the manager know he was going to lunch.

"Sam, be back in thirty minutes on the dot. You know the church crowd is coming in," the manager replied.

Kenyon realized that Carmello's name had changed under the witness protection program to Sam. Knowing that confirmed that the address he had found was indeed where they had him staying. Not wanting "Sam" to see him, Kenyon meticulously cleaned off the table and handed the waitress a fifty dollar bill. He watched as she dumped his dishes into the sink and hot water they had behind the counter. That was his way of making sure he could not be traced.

When he finally got outside of the diner, he looked around for "Sam", but he was no longer in the front. Kenyon decided to head to his truck and observe from there. As he walked across the street, he noticed Sam standing on the sidewalk talking to a man.

He turned the truck's front cameras on and headed in their direction. Kenyon almost crashed the truck when he saw Rome standing there. Quickly gaining control, he drove past them in awe. G's fiancé was standing with the eyewitness in her brother's case.

"Damn, this shit really chess not checkers," Kenyon thought to himself as he drove down the street.

To Be Continued...

Made in the USA
Middletown, DE
20 August 2019